CAPTAIN OF HER HEART

18th century: The ship *Golden Lady*, carrying rich treasure, is homeward bound for the bustling port of Liverpool when she is lured onto sandbanks and her captain, Jim Grenville, left for dead. He seeks shelter at Mother Redcap's tavern and is nursed back to health by her niece, Melany. Because of her deep love for Grenville, Melany tries to outwit Matt, the leader of the wreckers, and recover the treasure, although she realises that if she is successful she will lose Grenville . . .

MARION HARRIS

CAPTAIN OF HER HEART

Complete and Unabridged

LINFORD
Leicester

First published in Great Britain in 1976

First Linford Edition
published 2000

British Library CIP Data

Harris, Marion, *1925* –
Captain of her heart.—Large print ed.—
Linford romance library
1. Love stories
2. Large type books
I. Title
823.9′14 [F]

ISBN 0–7089–5777–3

Published by
F. A. Thorpe (Publishing)
Anstey, Leicestershire

Set by Words & Graphics Ltd.
Anstey, Leicestershire
Printed and bound in Great Britain by
T. J. International Ltd., Padstow, Cornwall

This book is printed on acid-free paper

1

Melany stood up defensively as the door of the small bedroom tucked away under the eaves of the Tavern opened. Her features relaxed as she saw it was only her Aunt who stood there.

'Well?'

Melany shook her head. 'Not yet.'

She sensed that her Aunt was growing increasingly concerned about the stranger who had come stumbling to their door and collapsed on the threshold before they had a chance to discover who he was. They had given him shelter believing him to be one of Matt's men. Later, when they had cleaned him up, they knew this was not so. This man was a gentleman not a ruffian. It was far more likely that he had been on board the *Golden Lady*, a ship Matt and his gang had plundered just a few days earlier.

The two women stood side by side looking down at the recumbent form of the man lying in the bed. The older woman was in her fifties, a short buxom figure in a dark dress. The lace-edged apron she wore was as snowy as the hair that peeped from beneath her red poke bonnet. It was rumoured that she never removed her bonnet, not even in bed at night, and it was from her distinctive headgear that her Tavern took its name.

'We can't leave him lying here much longer,' she warned her niece. Her lips tightened as her keen blue eyes noticed the flush that suffused Melany's cheeks and the protective way the girl laid a hand on the man's shoulder.

'But Aunt, he is ill. What else can we do but nurse him back to health.'

Mother Redcap moved closer, peering down at him speculatively. Stretching out her hand she lifted the lids of his eyes. The grey pupils beneath stared sightlessly into space.

'Oh, Aunt, you'll hurt him!'

The older woman chuckled harshly but withdrew her hand. 'Someone's already done that, my child.' She ran a calloused finger over the ugly bruise on the man's forehead. 'It's this blow to the temple that has done the damage.'

'It is gradually going down though, don't you think?' Melany looked hopefully at her Aunt.

Mother Redcap nodded. Then turning to the girl who still stood protectively by the bedside she said curtly, 'No point in feeling sorry for him, he's only some sailor, after all. Not even a fellow we know. Once he recovers he will be away. He'll have folks of his own to worry over him. Most likely he has a wife somewhere waiting for his return and children, too, I'll not doubt.'

She saw the girl's colour drain as she spoke and knew her suspicions were right. Melany was still young and impressionable and the mysterious stranger was capturing her fancy even before they had exchanged greetings.

In a voice more harsh than she

intended, Mother Redcap scolded, 'Away with you, my child. There's plenty of work below stairs to be attended to. There's pots to be washed and the chickens to be fed. It's too much for one pair of hands. He's hardly likely to disappear, not in the condition he is in at the moment, so come along and attend to your work. Time enough to sit by his bedside when everything is washed and scoured.'

Reluctantly Melany rose from the bedside and followed her Aunt down the narrow winding stairs to the large open parlour beneath. The beamed ceiling was hung with pewter drinking pots and oak settles lined the walls. In the wide hearth a small fire was burning.

'We need logs bringing in and the ashes cleaning away,' her Aunt told her, 'And when you've done that there's food to be got ready for tonight. Come girl, stop your mooning after that fellow upstairs. You're here to help me, remember, not to nurse a sick stranger.'

For two more days, whenever she could steal away from her work in the Tavern, Melany watched anxiously over the man who lay unconscious in the small bedroom tucked away under the eaves. From time to time she moistened his parched lips with a little water and brandy and bathed his bruised and fevered brow with a strip of linen wrung out in vinegar and water.

As she kept watch at the man's bedside, waiting for him to regain consciousness, Melany wondered who he might be. An enormous bruise covered his forehead where his assailant had struck him and, as he lay there with closed eyes, his face looked like a death mask yet the fiery shock of auburn hair and beard glinted and burned as the sun's rays caught it, giving it a life of its own.

His long inert frame filled the bed and showed that he was of powerful build. His broad shoulders, resting on the lace-edged pillow that she had taken from her own bed, and his muscular arms covered with a fine red hair, lying on top of the bedcovers, fully confirmed this fact.

Once or twice while she watched he had stirred restlessly and muttered, but, although she had bent low, Melany had not been able to catch what he had said. Her curiosity about him increased. He was one of the most handsome men she had ever seen and in repose his features, though broad and strong, seemed kind and compassionate. As she dabbed at his lips with water and brandy, she thrilled at their sensitivity. Here was a man whose kisses would be both passionate yet tender.

She studied his big powerful hands as they lay motionless on the bedcovers. The fingers were long and sensitive and although his hands denoted great strength they were well cared for and not calloused as were the hands of the men who usually frequented Mother Redcap's. This man, she felt sure, was a gentleman. Even though it seemed likely that he had come from the latest ship to be lured onto the sandbanks by Matt and his men he was no ordinary sailor. Perhaps he was a wealthy trader, she mused, returning home from foreign parts. There had been no papers about his person that gave any clue to his status but she had noted that his shirt though torn and soiled was of fine lawn and that his breeches and hose were both of good material.

She studied his hands again, lifting them from the bed-covers and cradling them in her own. He wore no rings so she could not say whether or not he had a wife, or even a family, waiting for word of his safe return. Gently she bent over him and let her own lips rest for one fleeting moment on his. As she did so he gave visible signs of life, as if her kiss had rekindled some dormant flame within him. The hand she held within her own stirred, then the clasp tightened. His lips parted in a smile as he stirred. She waited breathlessly but he seemed to sink back into his coma.

With a sigh, she carefully rearranged the covers and resumed her vigil.

Like her Aunt, Melany was anxious that the stranger should regain consciousness so that he could tell them who he was. It was urgent that he should do this before Matt and his gang next came to the Tavern.

Mother Redcap's Tavern stood isolated on a jutting prominence of sandstone that dominated the coastline and which was known locally as The Yellow Noses. The nearest villages of Wallasey, Liscard and Seacombe huddled several miles inland, sheltered from the wind and sea in their respective hollows. At high tide, the great breakers and rollers from the Irish sea would flood over the nearest sand dunes and high winds would sweep up the fine sand they left in their wake until it was piled in drifts some five to six feet high. For the most part the dunes were left free for the rabbits, weasels, stoats and foxes to run unmolested, free as air. The dunes were deserted, apart from

Matt and his gang. With one exception, the band of smugglers Matt led were ruffians who lived and worked on the wrong side of the law. With the aid of false lights they would lure the ships entering the narrow neck of the Mersey estuary, en route for Liverpool, onto the treacherous sandbanks. Meanwhile they hid themselves amidst the tangled mass of coarse grass and brambles that flourished between the sand dunes, watching the ship flounder. Then, just as she was about to capsize, they would descend in a horde to rob and plunder and to kill any who dared to resist.

There were some dozen or so men in Matt's gang. Dressed like fishermen, smoking stubby clay pipes, they looked a wild and unkempt lot. Many of them wore beards and on the faces of several were the scars that told of fights and knife wounds.

Matt was unquestionably their leader. His broad powerful shoulders and great height towered over the other men. When his lean square jaw, covered with a mat of short wiry black hair, was thrust out aggressively he was not a man to be trifled with, a fact most of them knew to their cost.

Melany hated them all . . . except Sammy. He was young fair haired and fresh complexioned and about Melany's own age. Like her he was an orphan. He had fallen in with Matt and his gang in Liverpool and Matt had decided to spare his life since he might prove to be a useful addition. Melany shuddered as she recalled Sammy's description of the wrecking of the *Golden Lady*, the first he had witnessed.

With Matt and his men he had huddled behind the sand dunes keeping watch for a ship they knew was due into Liverpool, waiting to spot it entering the estuary from the open sea.

They had lain there hour after hour, cold and uncomfortable, staring out into the darkness, until suddenly the ship had appeared, outlined on the horizon. As they watched the wind filled her great sails so that they bellied out. Above the noise of the waves breaking on the shore they could hear the swish of the spray as it swept over her bows. From somewhere inland two lights burned, but instead of guiding the ship into port like the friendly beacons they purported to be, they had lured her onto the treacherous sandbanks.

Matt had grabbed Sammy by the arm, hissing instructions into his ear.

'Now, when she beaches don't try to get aboard her. Wait until the crew begin to jump overboard. While they are still shocked from the coldness of the sea use your club. A good hard blow and then let the tide deal with them, but remember, no knives. Give 'em an extra blow with your club if you're not sure they're out. As I told you before, broken heads are common amongst seamen. Floating debris, spars crashing, masts falling — any of these can break a man's skull.

Once the men are dealt with, then board the ship and help in whatever way you can. Ask no questions, just do as the men instruct you and work fast. Daylight comes too fast when you're on a job like this. If anything goes wrong and the Customs men appear, or the seamen get the better of us — though that's unlikely — you know what to do. Make your own way to Mother Redcap's but remember, it's more than your life is worth to be caught or even to be seen. The signal is three hard raps and a light one, but that is only if things go wrong and it is unlikely that they will do so. One thing more, remember Sammy, if you are feeling squeamish about this affair just bear it in mind that no man has lived to tell tales about us.' He made a slashing motion with his hand and as he felt Matt's thick, calloused fingers across the skin of his throat Sammy had felt physically sick.

Concealing his revulsion he smiled feebly and in a strained voice said, 'I do understand Matt . . . you can count on me.'

'Good. Now just wait here. I'm going closer to see how things are.'

From behind the sand dunes, Sammy watched fascinated. As the moon rose high in the night sky, appearing suddenly from behind the clouds, the sand along the foreshore became a silver carpet. The wind still blew gustily but the sand and spray it threw up became a glittering cascade of jewels in the silver light that enveloped the world. Breakers no longer crashed on the shore. The waters twirled and twisted as if undecided whether to come on inshore or to recede. A wave more deliberate than the others would boldly fling a cascade of water towards the shore, then an unseen force would pull back the water. Little by little the waters were receding, leaving damp dappled patterns in their wake, its very wetness beautiful in the moonlight.

The ship was clearer now, no longer just a dark silhouette against an even darker background but a privateer with billowing sails and proudly flying flags, gracefully riding the sea. As he watched, she seemed to shudder, as if aware that the light she had been following, the lights believed to have come from Liverpool, had been from the wrong shore.

'They're trying to change course,' Sammy muttered and in his heart he hoped they might succeed. For one wild moment he thought of running away. He looked round him, there were shadows everywhere. Moonlight made inland seem more sinister and eerie than the darkness had done. Strangely fascinated he watched the ship trying to change course in mid-stream. She had already sailed over the central channel of the Mersey. Sandbanks and reefs filled the mouth of the river which was why most ships waited until daylight, before negotiating upstream and into harbour.

From where he waited, Sammy had been able to make out the shape of men running to and fro on the top deck. As he watched, he saw the sails suddenly lose their tautness and sag against the night sky as the sailors prepared to lower them.

Perhaps they are going to anchor in midstream until daybreak, he thought. This would defeat all Matt's plans. Suddenly as if at the command of Matt and his men, a tremendous gust of wind came sweeping up the estuary, tossing the ship like a cork.

With nightmare speed, the privateer was washed up onto a sandbank and Matt and his men were rushing down to the beach. As they ran they brandished their clubs, shouting and yelling to each other. The ship lay on her side, like a wounded animal, her giant spars parallel with the shore. The wind had dropped, the sea was rapidly receding and very soon she would be high and dry. He felt dazed. He could hardly believe it was all really happening. Matt and his men had reached her by now and even from where he stood Sammy could see they were using their clubs freely. Then he saw Matt pause in his evil work to look round and he knew he had been missed. Making a supreme effort Sammy pulled himself together and began to run over the wet sand to where the wreck lay. At that moment a man ran past him, heading inland. He heard Matt call out, commanding him to stop the man. Knowing Matt was watching, Sammy swung his club at the running figure. Fear leant strength to his blows, although the man was bigger than him and ready to defend himself. He swung the club wildly until the fellow lay unconscious at his feet. When he realised what he had done, Sammy was overcome with horror.

Afterwards, when he had come back to Mother Redcap's with Matt and the others, Sammy had told Melany about his experience. He had not boasted or bragged of his achievements as the others had done. He had confided in her because he needed to expurgate the deed from his mind, because he was sick to the soul by what he had done.

Melany had held Sammy's hand and

expressed her concern but she couldn't help him. Melany feared Matt just as Sammy did, just as his men did, probably even more so. When he reached out his massive calloused hand to caress her bare arm or stroke her long black hair as she poured his ale, she would feel goose pimples rising on her neck and cold trickles of sweat creeping down inside her gown. The only person who didn't fear Matt was her Aunt, Mother Redcap.

2

When at last Jim Grenville opened his eyes he found himself in a small low-ceilinged room. The walls were whitewashed and bright curtains hung at the small mullioned window. The bed he lay in was a four-poster with curtains of the same gay material as those at the window. Wonderingly, he passed a hand over his eyes and as he did so his fingers touched the cloth resting on his right temple. He tried to recall where he was and what had happened. The room was unfamiliar and the window too high and small for him to see through it. Cautiously he pulled himself up in bed. His bones ached and he trembled as though he were suffering from an ague. He found he was clad in a nightshirt of white calico, and as he examined it he was alarmed to discover that it was a lady's with lace ruffles at the neck and sleeves.

'What has happened to me?' he said aloud. 'Am I dreaming all this. Will I waken to find myself in my own cabin, rolling on a high sea.'

As he spoke the door opened and a young woman entered. She was about nineteen or twenty, tall and slim. Against her gown of bright green with its white lace insertion at the throat, her skin appeared a delicate cream. Her jet black hair, caught back from her face with a green ribbon, hung in glistening coils at the nape of her neck. Her features, though small, were well formed and delicate. Her large eyes were a deep soft brown. As she approached the bed her lips parted in a smile that showed her even, white teeth, and in a voice that was low and husky she said, 'You are awake at last. I am so glad. It has seemed so long.'

Grenville could only stare. The awakening in the strange room and the sudden appearance of this lovely girl bewildered his weakened senses.

Putting a cool, smooth hand on his brow, she said, 'Lie back again on your pillow. I will fetch you a warm drink and then we will talk. Only for a little while, mind you. You have been very ill and you must be kept quiet.'

Unprotesting, Grenville allowed her to slip an arm under his shoulders and gently re-arrange his pillow. He closed his eyes and tried to piece together the puzzle. The strange room, this unknown girl and the fact that he had been ill and must be kept quiet. Thinking made his head ache. With a sigh, he lay quite still, content to listen for the sound of her returning footsteps.

The milk she brought him was warm and laced with rum. He drank it thirstily. His throat was rough and sore, his tongue felt swollen and his lips were dry and cracked.

'Now,' she said, taking the empty glass and gently wiping his mouth. 'I'll fix the pillow so that you are a little higher in the bed and then we can talk.'

He listened while she told him how, three nights before, he had arrived on the doorstep of the Tavern in a bedraggled state. His bewilderment increased when she said he had collapsed on the threshold before he could tell them who he was, or where he had come from or how he had been injured.

'But where am I?' he asked. 'And who are you?'

'This is Mother Redcap's Tavern and I am her niece. Melany.'

'Mother Redcap's!' Jim Grenville sat bolt upright.

'Do you mean I have been lying here for three days and no one in Liverpool has been informed?'

Melany stared solemnly at him, then said quietly in her husky voice, 'We had no idea who you were. The night you came here there was a ship wrecked higher up the coast. We were not sure if you had been washed ashore from her or not. You carried no papers. Your clothes were in rags and we had no way of finding out who you were.'

With a groan Grenville buried his face in his hands. 'Of course,' he said bitterly, 'it's all coming back to me now. I remember everything. The wreck . . . being washed up . . . the ship being ransacked . . . struggling this far and then . . . ' he shook his head and his grey eyes had a bewildered expression.

'It's no good . . . I can't remember any more,' he flopped back onto the pillow exhausted.

'You collapsed when you reached here,' Melany said quietly. 'You have been here three days and this is the first time you have regained consciousness. Have you friends or relatives in Liverpool, someone you would like me to get in touch with for you?'

He uncovered his face and his grey eyes were feverishly bright. 'Yes, yes . . . that is it. You must help me.' He leaned forward as he spoke, took one of her hands in his and stared eagerly into her dark brown eyes.

'Promise me you'll help me, Melany. Tell me I can depend on you,' he pleaded.

For what seemed to him like eternity she scrutinised his face, her dark eyes giving no clue to her thoughts.

'Please,' he begged her.

She patted his hand reassuringly. 'I'll do all I can to help you,' she told him.

'Listen,' he began feverishly. 'You must get a message to Liverpool . . . to Cornelius Tobin. Have you ever heard of him?'

'Everyone hereabouts has heard of Cornelius Tobin. He is the greatest shipowner in these parts . . . what is he to you?'

Grenville smiled bitterly. 'He might one day have been my father-in-law. Now, he will probably be my enemy for life.'

Melany looked at him questioningly.

'Why do you say that?'

Grenville peered round the small room. 'Are we safe to talk here? Can anyone overhear what I am going to tell you?'

Melany shook her head. 'My Aunt is attending to customers downstairs and there is no one else in the house. I must not stay long. My Aunt expects me to help serve the ale and the food.'

'This won't take long. I must tell you and you must help me as quickly as possible. You said a few minutes ago that a ship was wrecked the night I came here. Tell me, was it called *The Golden Lady*?'

Melany's hand flew to her lips as if to hold back her cry of astonishment. 'I was right then, you were on board her.'

He nodded grimly. 'Do you know who fixed the lights to lure us onto the sandbank? Do you know who the men were who wrecked and plundered her and killed my crew?' His anger rose until he was shouting in a hoarse strained whisper.

'Quiet, quiet!' Melany entreated. Swiftly she crossed to the window and closed it. 'Speak quietly,' she cautioned as she returned and seated herself on the bed. 'I may know the men you speak of but many strange sailors and the like come here at all hours of the night and day . . . many after I am abed of nights.'

'If I can lay hands on the scoundrels, and they have not been brought to justice, I'll strangle every man of them myself, with my own hands.'

Panting, he lay back on his pillow, a haggard figure with fever bright eyes and sunken cheeks under a fiery, unruly mop of hair.

She smoothed his damp brow with gentle fingers. 'You are fevered,' she warned. 'Lie quiet and rest and we will talk again later when you are calmer.'

Impatiently he shook her hand away. 'We must talk now and you must listen to me. You have promised to help me. I was the Captain of that ship. The thought they had killed me e blow they dealt me, thanks ur tender nursing, has not proved la n. I must have lain on the ground after they had given me up for dead. I went back on board and discovered the destruction and havoc they had done. Not only had they clubbed down every man aboard but they had taken my cargo — the wines, spirits, bales of silk, tobacco and spices I was bringing back from foreign lands. They had even broken open my own personal sea chest. In it was a fortune in silver and gold and jewels. A king's ransom. I had guarded it personally, night and day, throughout the voyage. No man on board knew its value though many suspected what it might contain. Now, I find myself lying here in this strange bedroom, alone and ill, penniless and dependent upon strangers for food and drink, whilst someone else reaps that rich reward.'

Exhausted and bitter with self pity he lay back panting for breath.

'But how did you come by it?'

With an effort he roused himself to go on with his story. 'It was buried on an island, far away in the Pacific. The map showing its location had been entrusted to Cornelius Tobin by one of his Captains of one of his vessels as he lay dying. This man after capturing the treasure from a French frigate had buried it on the island for fear of being attacked on the way home. Cornelius Tobin commissioned me to find the island and return with the treasure. My reward was to be the hand of his daughter. Now,' he smiled bitterly, 'my dreams are over. Instead of a wedding there will be a censure for losing both the *Golden Lady* and the treasure.'

Melany remained silent, her dark eyes unfathomable. Then, as if thinking aloud, she said, 'But surely, if the girl loves you . . . '

Grenville smiled grimly. 'If your father were Cornelius Tobin would you defy him to marry a penniless Sea Captain who had lost his ship to the wreckers when he was almost within sight of his own quayside?'

Melany's eyes were steady as they met his. 'That would depend on the man himself,' she said. Rising from his side she crossed to the window and standing with her back towards him asked, 'What is it you want me to do?'

Grenville sighed. 'I don't know. When I first began to talk to you I had the idea that you could get a message to Cornelius Tobin. I wanted you to tell him that *The Golden Lady* had been attacked by wreckers off the Wallasey coast and that his Captain, Jim Grenville, lay at Mother Redcap's injured and needing help and money. Now I am not so sure. Perhaps it would be better to let him think I was dead.'

'That would be a coward's way out, Captain Grenville.' She spoke softly, keeping her face turned from him. 'And what of his daughter . . . would you have her pine and weep for a man she thought dead while all the time he lies in hiding.'

Grenville sighed. 'Perhaps you're right. Even if Tobin will not believe my story, Corrina will. Have you ever met her, Melany?'

The girl laughed gently, without rancour, as she answered, 'How would I meet a fine lady like Mistress Tobin?'

As if realising the foolishness of his question Grenville made no reply. Dreamily he said, 'Every night while I've been away I've thought of her and prayed for her safety. I had a wonderful vision of my homecoming. I would sail proudly into Liverpool with flags flying. Cornelius Tobin and Corrina would be on the quayside to meet me in their fine carriage . . . '

'This is no time for such dreams,' Melany interrupted sharply.

Ignoring her, Grenville went on, 'I would tell them of the success of my trip and present the great chest of gold and jewels to Cornelius Tobin. Then Corrina's eyes — they're vivid blue, like Larkspur in summer — would light up as her father suggested I should ride with them back to their house. He would invite me to wait with Corrina in the carriage while he made an inspection of *The Golden Lady*. Once we were alone in the seclusion of the carriage she would tell me what I've waited so long to hear.'

Melany turned back to the window so that Grenville would not see the unhappiness in her face or the tears of jealousy that filled her eyes.

'When the seas were dark and heavy,' Grenville went on, 'and we seemed further from home than ever, my dreams became even greater flights of fancy. I could hear the church bells ring out over Liverpool, and see Corrina, her golden hair covered with a film of white veiling, walking down the aisle on her father's arm to where I stood waiting near the altar. Or, I'd think of her settled in our own home, waiting for my return from some foreign land and the presents of silk and jewels that I would be bringing her.' He gave a half smile at his memories. 'How her eyes would have lighted up had she seen the treasure I had on board *The Golden Lady* before the wreckers plundered her. Now I am penniless! How can I expect her to marry me now, even if her father would consent.'

Gently Melany placed her slim hand over his, 'You set too great a store by wealth,' she told him. 'Love should surpass such materialistic things.'

'Fine words, fine sentiments.' He shook his head gloomily. 'That fortune was to have been my redemption. Without it I were better dead.'

'It is the fever and your weak state that makes you think and talk like this. I will cross to Liverpool this very day and seek out Cornelius Tobin and tell him of your plight. How will that suit you?'

Grenville's grey eyes shone with gratitude. 'You'd do that much for me?'

'Only if you lie back again on those

pillows and eat the broth I am going to fetch for you now. This is important. If my Aunt should come in say nothing of where I have gone nor mention who you are. Whatever happens she mustn't learn that you are from the wreck. Understand?'

'But why . . . '

'No questions. When I return from Liverpool we will talk again. In the meantime let my Aunt think you have regained consciousness but that you are still too weak to talk. Unless you promise me that you will do this it is not safe for me to leave your side.'

3

Liverpool was astir. The narrow cobbled streets were crowded. The quayside was a scene of bustle. A slave ship lay at anchor ready to unload its human cargo. People gathered near the Goree Piazas to watch the long line of blacks, being brought from it to be sold. They moved in a long file, hampered by the heavy chains, which bound the ankles of each man to those of the men in front and behind him. They shuffled along, dirty and smelling, all ages — even young boys — rolling their eyes piteously as if their souls called out for deliverance.

Here and there in the line a buxom negress was chained loosely to her husband; most of these women carried a child in arms. They had either refused to leave their man when he was captured, or they had themselves been captured and would now be sold as house-slaves. The blacks were chained to the iron rings set in the walls while the auctioneers set up their stands. A space was cleared for the buyers to come and view them. The afternoon was early and the sale would not commence for at least another hour. Meanwhile the blacks shivered piteously. After the close stuffiness they had known on board during the last six months they felt the cold keenly.

Their only salvation lay in the fact that few of them would remain in the bleakness of Liverpool. Apart from a few young boys — Blackamoors who would be purchased by men of wealth as a present to a lady of fashion — they would be sold and then transported to America. There they would work in the British colonies, on the sugar, tobacco or cotton plantations. The sun there would be warm like that of their native West Africa.

But now they were herded and chained, like so many black cattle, into an open air market. Each would be poked and prodded by buyers, their finer points enhanced by the auctioneers, their deficiencies glossed over. When the bidding commenced each prime male would fetch sums of up to one hundred pounds. The more sickly amongst them might only raise a single bid of a pound or two. Yet, one thing was certain, every black dog among them would change owners. And then they would be re-shipped — another load of human merchandise.

Meanwhile Liverpool gazed upon them with curious and speculative eyes, sizing each man and boy up at his monetary value. For to Liverpool, slaves were a valuable trading asset. Few people could see anything wrong with the practice. After all it had the sanction of Parliament; and how could a race who spoke only in gibberish have human feelings.

It was to such a scene that Melany came, seeking Cornelius Tobin. As the small fishing boat, carrying some fifteen people from the Wallasey side of the Mersey, pulled into the harbour, the blacks were just disappearing from sight up the cobbled roadway.

Lifting her gown carefully — for it was her best green silk — in one hand, Melany allowed the owner of the boat to help her ashore. She sounded him as to the time of his return, before tripping cautiously over the cobbles and making for the cluster of houses near St. Nicholas Church.

The larger of these houses Jim Grenville had told her belonged to Cornelius Tobin. He conducted his office affairs from it so she would be sure either to find him there or learn of his whereabouts.

She gazed around; overawed by the bustle and crowds near the waterfront. Great ships lay at anchor in the pool. Some were waiting to draw alongside the harbour and discharge their cargoes. Others were waiting for the change of tide so that they might once more take to the high seas and, with sails bellying, set out for distant lands.

Everywhere there were sea-faring men; some wore their hair drawn back in a tight pigtail, others had it close cropped. A few tried to accost her, but with head averted, lips tightly sealed, and her skirts clutched in one hand, she hurried past them; her high heels ringing out a sharp staccato on the cobbled road.

Reaching Tobin's house she hesitated. It semed improper to venture to the great imposing front door and demand to see so eminent a man as Cornelius Tobin. She wondered if any of the side doors gave entrance to his office apartments.

While she stood in the roadway, uncertain of what to do, there was a clatter on the cobbles behind her as a gentleman, wrapped in a voluminous riding cloak, astride a magnificent grey horse, swept up the drive. Seeing her he drew rein, and doffing his plumed hat, asked if he might be of some service.

Melany told him she wished to see Cornelius Tobin but was undecided which was the right door to use.

His green eyes were cold and calculating as he studied her flushed face. 'Cornelius Tobin is not at home,' he told her. 'I met him not five minutes since, with a party of Liverpool business men, studying the blacks being put up for sale in the Goree Piazas. If you hurry you might be able to speak to him before the actual sale commences.'

Melany thanked him for the information. 'Can you direct me to the place of the sale,' she asked.

For a moment he hesitated.

'Gad, I would like to show you the way. Unfortunately, I am already late for an appointment with Miss Corrina Tobin, and dare not risk offending her by further delay.'

'No indeed. Of course not. I was not suggesting that you should accompany me.' Melany felt most embarrassed by the misunderstanding. 'I merely request that you point out the shortest way and tell me how long it will take me to walk there.'

'Walk! You have no carriage?'

'No, Sir. I have come from Wallasey by boat and I am only here for an hour or so. I have private business, on behalf of a friend, with Cornelius Tobin. I have been entrusted with a message that I must at all costs deliver to him personally. If you will be good enough to direct me. I have very little time before my boat returns.'

'But you are such a little thing to be wandering about the streets alone. There are many rough sailors, and the like, loafing about these parts, who would not think twice of accosting a young and pretty girl like you.' His green eyes stared boldly.

'I am quite able to take care of myself, Sir. Please give me the necessary directions. Otherwise I must leave you and ask the way of some stranger. Maybe,' she allowed a smile to cross her face, 'one of those scurrilous seamen of which you speak.'

The horseman laughed. 'You have a pretty tongue and a forceful manner. Curse upon it that my appointment with Miss Corrina keeps me from accompanying you. However, your way is easy. There should be no fear of you getting lost, even though the streets are so crowded today.'

Unused to the cobbled streets her feet were soon tired and aching. Several times she wondered whether she should engage one of the horse drawn carriages, that were plying for hire along the narrow roads. Fear that the cabby might not take her to her destination, and doubtful as to whether she would have enough money to pay him if he did, made her resolve to make her way there on foot.

News of the impending sale of slaves had spread, and business men jostled with pedlars, seamen and fishwives. Expensively dressed nobility looked over the wares. Some were there to buy in their own right, but most of the rich who dabbled in the slave trade did so through their agents. A few prosperous merchants were there accompanied by their ladies. They rode in fine carriages driven by liveried coachmen. An attendant on foot cleared a path through the crowds in order that her Ladyship might view the blackamoors that were for sale, and take her choice.

Desperately Melany squeezed her way between the crowds, enquiring frequently from those men she thought might be slave-traders, if any of them could tell her where to find Cornelius Tobin.

At last she was told he had been seen near the auctioneer's stand and was directed towards it. The crowds here were much denser and soon she was hot, flustered and tired from pushing between the closely packed people. Desperate with frustration she stepped out over the evil smelling gutters that were choked with refuse, and began to run along the roadway itself.

Suddenly, a carriage drew up almost on top of her and a voice hailed her to stop. The magnificence of the carriage stunned her senses. A handsome crest was engraved on the door panel and the high wheels were decorated with intricate gold and crimson scroll work. The coachman and footman, resplendent in crimson and gold livery, rode in front, handling the reins of the two sleek black horses. In front of the horses' heads a liveried youth, armed with a silver headed club, cleared a way through the crowds.

From the carriage window a face appeared.

With relief Melany recognised the man she had met outside Cornelius Tobin's house. He had discarded his riding cloak and was now resplendent in white knee breeches, and a long black velvet coat edged at the wrists and neck with fine white lace. As he stepped from the carriage, great silver buckles glittered on his shoes, and she saw he carried a pair of pure white kid gloves.

Fixing a monocle to his left eye he

assumed a haughty manner and tapping Melany on the shoulder with a silver topped cane he said, in refined tones, 'Are you still looking for Cornelius Tobin.'

Breathlessly she nodded her head. Her dark eyes shining with relief at finding someone whom she felt would help her in her quest. Then she became aware of the cold, scrutinising stare of a fashionably dressed lady sitting in the carriage. Melany raised a hand to straighten her bonnet, which had been pushed askew while she jostled with the crowds. Her cheeks flushed painfully as she realised how dishevelled and travel stained she must appear.

As she stared at the woman she had a vivid impression of smooth cool beauty in a rich blue velvet cloak that covered a shimmering gown of pale blue silk. Corrina's eyes were as blue as Jim Grenville had described them, and her lovely golden hair framed her oval features like a glittering halo. She wore it dressed in the height of fashion.

It was arranged high and waved in the front, then drawn back to hang in golden coils around her tiny ears and milk white neck.

Smothering a genteel yawn behind a dainty silk gloved hand, Corrina murmured, 'Shall we drive on my Lord Pendleton. I am most anxious to view this Blackamoor you have spoken of, before the sale commences.'

'Please, please wait.' In desperation Melany caught at Pendleton's arm. 'Perhaps Miss Tobin would permit me to have a few words with her.' She looked appealingly into the blue eyes that started coldly back at her.

'I understood your business was with my father,' Corrina said frigidly.

'Yes, yes, it was; but it concerned both of you. I was asked to convey a message to your father, yet I feel sure that if the sender had thought, for one moment, that I should have an opportunity to speak to you, he would have wished me to convey a message to you also.'

'Really.' The blue eyes showed faint interest. 'I should have thought it unlikely that we had any mutual acquaintances.'

Ignoring the snub, Melany looked from Corrina to Pendleton.

'I think I had better . . . that is . . . ', she paused awkwardly.

Corrina re-arranged the folds of her blue, velvet cloak as she said testily, 'You are quite free to divulge any information you may be carrying. My Lord Pendleton is a close friend of mine and, I can assure you, he is quite trustworthy.'

Melany bridled at her tone. A hot colour suffused her face and neck.

'I am quite sure of that. I thought maybe you yourself would prefer to hear the message in private.'

Corrina lowered her lovely golden lashes in a bored manner.

'I thought you said there was no direct message for me. Is it something you wish me to tell my father?'

'No, not really. If I am unable to

find your father I should of course be grateful if you would deliver a message for me.'

'Quick, wench! I am in a hurry and both I, and Lord Pendleton, are tired of your dalliance. From whom do you bring a message?'

Looking straight into the blue eyes Melany said, 'From Jim Grenville!'

With a start Corrina sat bolt upright in her carriage. Her face paled and her small white teeth bit onto her lower lip, as if to prevent a scream.

'But he's dead! What trumped up tale is this. Who are you and where do you come from?'

Briefly Melany told Corrina how, three nights earlier, Jim Grenville had collapsed at Mother Redcap's door, and had been taken in and nursed back to life. She explained that his first thoughts, on regaining consciousness, had been for Corrina and her father, and how upset he was by the realisation that he had lost both his ship and the treasure he had carried on board.

At the end of her recital Melany waited breathlessly for Corrina to speak.

Corrina's eyes were hard, her lips a thin tight line in the beautiful oval face as she said in an icy voice, 'I have no time for failures; neither has my father. You waste your time seeking him. Such a message, as you have to convey, will mean nothing to him; in fact, it will only incite him to even greater anger against Captain Grenville.'

'Come, my dear,' languidly Pendleton took up the argument, 'You are being hard on our little friend. It is no fault of hers that she is the bearer of bad news. As for your father's anger being incited by such news, surely he will be glad to hear that his Captain is alive, and stands a chance of recovery. From gossip I've heard your father held Captain Grenville in high esteem and he was not the only one.' He laughed waggishly and patted her smooth cheek. 'Come my pretty, admit that the handsome Captain had won for himself a place in your affections.'

'Captain Grenville believed that had he been successful in his recent venture he would have been granted Miss Corrina's hand in marriage,' burst out Melany, her face hot with anger at the reception of her news.

'Aha!' Pendleton raised his brows in mock surprise. 'What dark secret is this, which the sea has thrown up.'

'Quiet, you fool!' Angrily Corrina stamped her foot. 'This wench prattles of something about which she knows nothing. She echoes the hysterical ravings of a Captain who loses his ship when within sight of his own port. These tales of gold and riches, which he claims to have brought home with him, but conveniently lost to the wreckers, mean nothing to me. Return to your fine friend, wench, and tell him from me that a Captain who loses his ship and his cargo deserves to lose his rank.'

'Come, my dear Corrina, aren't you being rather hard on the poor sailor? His first thoughts were for you, remember. You must have given him some encouragement. In his condition your message might easily cause a relapse.'

'Be quiet, my Lord Pendleton.' Corrina's cheeks were flushed with anger. Her voice was sharp as she tried to mask the fury raging inside her.

'I say again, this man is nothing to me. Am I to feel responsible for the well being of every Captain who commands one of my father's ships. Remember, he has some twenty-six ships plying for the high seas, besides the *Golden Lady*, which is now a miserable wreck. Am I then to feel myself committed to all their captains?'

'Not unless they are all as young and as handsome as Jim Grenville is reputed to be.' Pendleton smiled teasingly. 'Let us ask this maid if he is as handsome, and debonair, as rumour states. I warrant she has an eye that could tell a pleasing gentleman if she saw one. Well, my dear?'

Melany looked from Pendleton's sardonically smirking face to Corrina's tight lipped one. Any help she might have expected from Corrina was evidently not forthcoming. Far better, she reflected, had she spent her time looking for Cornelius Tobin. Whatever his feelings over the loss of his ship might be, she felt sure she would have received a fairer hearing from him than she was receiving from Corrina.

Resignedly she turned from the carriage. 'My time is short. In a very few minutes I must find the boat that is to take me back to Wallasey or I shall be stranded.'

'Pity, pity,' murmured Pendleton, smoothing on his kid gloves. 'No doubt the Captain will be eagerly awaiting your return.'

Melany turned again to Corrina, and stepping up onto the foot-plate of the carriage, implored, 'Reconsider your decision, I beg you. Captain Grenville counts so much on your help and intervention with your father on his behalf. It was not his fault that he became a victim of the wreckers. His only fault lay in his eagerness to be near you, to bring you the fine gifts and treasure he had aboard for you. If he had not attempted to navigate the channel in the dark, he would never have been lured ashore. He should have lain safely at anchor, at the mouth of the river, and sailed in with the morning tide. If that had happened he, and not Lord Pendleton, would be riding with you now.'

For one moment Melany thought Corrina would strike her. The blue eyes that Grenville had so poetically described as larkspur blue, became slits of blue ice. The daintily gloved hand rose in the air as two spots of colour flamed in Corrina's cheeks. 'You slut!' she screamed in a hard shrill voice. Then without her demeanour changing she called sharply to her coachman, 'Drive on.'

With a sudden jolt the great carriage lurched forward and Melany was thrown from her precarious position, on the foot-plate. She would have fallen into the muddy street had not a passer-by caught her arm and steadied her.

Dazedly, she thanked him, then with a heavy heart made her way back to the quayside. The fishing boat was waiting to take her back to Wallasey and to Grenville.

4

Arriving back at Mother Redcap's, Melany was relieved to find Jim Grenville asleep. As the boat, bringing her from Liverpool, had rocked through the swirling grey Mersey, she had turned over, in her mind, the interview with Corrina Tobin. She dreaded having to tell Grenville that her efforts, on his behalf, had been useless. He must never know that Corrina despised him for losing his ship, and the treasure he had had on board, to the wreckers. Nor must he ever know that, not only had she no intention of awaiting his return, but, she was not even interested in his welfare. To break such news to him at the moment would only delay his recovery. Desperately Melany tried to reason what was the best thing for her to do. Should she concoct a story, telling only half the truth of her encounter. Or, should she say she had not had the opportunity to speak to either Cornelius Tobin or his daughter. If she told Jim Grenville that he would probably beg her to try again to see them, and tell them of his whereabouts. Perhaps, if she had seen Cornelius Tobin himself her reception would have been different. Yet it had been Corrina's help Jim Grenville had been counting on.

Finding Grenville asleep gave her a brief respite from the unpleasant duty which lay before her. Slipping away to her own room she changed from her green silk gown into her everyday homespun. As she hung the green dress back in the closet she saw that the hem was badly bedraggled and splashed with mud, as a result of her journey through Liverpool's streets. Ruefully, she decided that the afternoon had been a sad one in every way, and carefully folding her dress, she left the repairs, and cleaning, until she had more time to attend to them.

Mother Redcap was busy serving meals, and drinks, to a crowded room. Without waiting to be asked Melany stepped forward and began to take orders from the waiting customers, who were impatiently stamping on the floor and demanding service. Between serving tankards of porter and home brewed ale — the rich dark liquid they brewed themselves, she found time to ask her Aunt how their invalid had been.

'Poor man, he seems low in spirits,' said Mother Redcap, pausing to push back a strand of white hair beneath her red poke bonnet. 'After you went out I looked in on him to see if there was anything he wanted. He said he was quite comfortable but he seemed disinclined to talk. He said he felt weak and thought he would try and sleep.'

'He's sleeping now. I looked in just before I came downstairs.'

The old woman nodded her head thoughtfully. 'I'd rather his room than his company, us being as busy as we are. It takes all our time serving here. Not that I'd turn any man, woman, or child away when he was sick,' she ended hastily, catching sight of the disapproval on Melany's face.

'I promise you, Aunt, he shall be no trouble to you. I will continue nursing him myself, after I've finished helping you.'

Mother Redcap looked shrewdly at Melany. Was the girl in love with the red-headed sailor, she wondered. Many men had been brought to their doors after a wreck, and sheltered with no questions asked, but never before could she remember Melany having showed the slightest interest in any of them. Come to that, Melany showed little interest in any of the men, and they were many and varied, who frequented the tavern. True, she always had a civil tongue in her head for them. She would smile at their sallies and jests, and reply to their chaff. If they became rough, in either their manners or talk, she quickly silenced them with a cold stare. Strangely enough, the men seemed to understand her attitude, and to like her the more for it. True, a few of the younger, and bolder, ones had persisted with their attentions. Usually when this happened some of the older, and quieter, types warned them to behave and to stop pestering her.

Mother Redcap sighed complacently. She supposed she should be glad that Melany adopted this attitude, otherwise trouble could have resulted in the past. Men inflamed by drink, and talk of wild doings, were apt to be hard to handle; especially when there was a pretty girl around the place. Even though she was blood relation to Melany, she had to admit that the girl was both pretty in her face and in her ways.

There was only one thing which rankled her, Melany did not encourage confidences. With intrigue all around her Mother Redcap often felt the need to talk over her fears and doubts about some of the men who frequented her tavern. Many were the lawless tales she overheard, as she served food and drink, and likewise, so must Melany. But never a word of gossip passed Melany's lips. It was as if she was deaf to the murmuring around her, and blind to the queer happenings, in, and around, the tavern.

Yet, Mother Redcap reasoned, Melany could not be all that blind to the true facts. Many a time she had bidden the girl to set the weather vane 'fair' or 'cloudy' as suited the occasion. From force of circumstances she had explained to her that it was a signal to those of their customers who might be carrying contraband.

If the vane was set 'cloudy' it served as a warning that there were customs men inside the tavern. If it was set 'fair' then they knew it was safe for them to enter.

Melany must also be aware of the additional activity that went on in, and around, the tavern when a wreck was discovered. And, although she was always safe within her room before any of the wreckers crept in through the many secret entrances, she must know of their movements.

Speculatively, Mother Redcap watched Melany scurrying about refilling tankards, and chaffing blithely with the men; and wondered just how much the girl knew, or guessed. She felt it would be something of a relief to gossip with Melany, and lighten her own mind of doubts and fancies.

Once again Mother Redcap's thoughts turned to the red-headed stranger lying upstairs. Who was he; had he come from the *Golden Lady*?

Matt, who had led the wreckers that night, had told her that not a man had escaped; and, for some reason, she had not told Matt of the stranger's presence. Now she was in something of a quandary. He had laid in the small room above the tavern for three days and nights, and to tell Matt now would only incite his anger for having kept the matter a secret for so long. Not that she feared Matt. It was just that he was one of her best customers and she had no wish to rile him. He had such a fiendish temper when aroused.

With a shudder she recalled the anger he had shown with young Sammy, who had missed the rest of the wreckers the night the *Golden Lady* had come aground, and had turned up at the tavern some half an hour after them.

Sammy had given the code signal, in raps, on the front door and Matt himself had gone to open it. Once the boy was within the house and the massive oak door had swung shut, and had been securely bolted, Matt had rounded on him.

Sammy's explanation, that after the wreck had been grounded he had been too stunned and frightened to do very much, cut no ice with Matt. A bold and fearless man himself, roused to action by danger, he could understand neither fear, nor bewilderment, in another.

He listened impatiently, his heavy lips curling in a sneer, as Sammy related how, when Matt had called to him to strike down the man running from the *Golden Lady*, it had taken all his will power to do so. He watched with undisguised contempt while Sammy paused in his story to wipe away the beads of sweat from above his eyes, at the thought of the horrors his tale conjured up to him.

'Did you finish the fellow off?' Matt demanded harshly. 'Don't lie to me, lad. As soon as day breaks you can come back again to the wreck with me and identify the body.'

Sammy looked at him in horror and in a voice faint with anguish, said, 'It would be no good, the second time I struck him he collapsed and rolled backwards into the sea.'

Observing that some of the other men were furtively watching them, and were probably able to make out what their argument was about, Matt let the matter drop. It was evident from his subsequent treatment of Sammy that he thought the boy a fool, and a weak-livered fool at that.

In her motherly way Mother Redcap had tried to atone to the lad for Matt's rough treatment. Although he had not asked for it, she pushed a plate of home cured ham into his hand, and laced his glass of ale with a generous dash of rum.

Sammy smiled up at her, gratefully, but seemed too scared to voice his appreciation.

With a sigh Mother Redcap brought her thoughts back to her customers. She felt sorry for Sammy. The wreckers, who worked and drank with Matt, were tough men to compete with. Any show of softness on the part of any of them would be dealt with by Matt in a ruthless manner. Provided such lawlessness was not enacted under her roof she could do little to prevent it. It frequently troubled her when a face she had grown accustomed to serving with her own home brewed ale suddenly appeared no more at the tavern. Her discreet enquiries would be met with either evasive answers or complete silence.

She had been able to warn a few men that Matt, and his gang, were after their blood. Once or twice she had even managed to conceal them in the tavern, in one, or the other, of the many secret hiding places. There they had remained, safe from Matt and his men, until such time as they could slip away to Liverpool. There they were able to join up with some ship sailing to the East, or to the Americas. Of these men she sometimes heard rumours; some of the bolder ones even ventured to return, after an absence of many years. For the most part, however, she was powerless to help them if they incurred Matt's displeasure.

She served them with ale and porter, home-cured ham and eggs, and when the Customs men were in the vicinity she gave fair warning. To those who cared to pay well she was free with her help, and would allow them the use of the tavern's secret entrances, exits, and hide-outs. And, as all had learnt, she was close with her tongue. A secret shared with Mother Redcap was a secret well hidden. Whether it was the hiding, or disposing, of contraband, or dodging the press gang, she could be trusted. In return she asked only that her own privacy be respected. If, for some reason, a certain hiding place was not available to a regular customer, then he must neither ask questions nor pry. Help she would give freely, whenever it was within her power to do so.

At the moment she was deeply concerned over the red haired man lying in the room above them. He was not one of the local wreckers, nor did he appear to be a man trying to escape the press gang. His face, even though ravaged by illness, was from a finer mould than that of the usual seaman who took refuge in her house. That there was something worrying him she had no doubt. A sense of foreboding filled Mother Redcap.

There was something ominous about his arrival being so near the time when the *Golden Lady* was wrecked.

As soon as opportunity afforded she intended to question him on the matter. After all, it was in her house that he was lying, and therefore, he owed her an explanation. She felt that Melany knew something that she was keeping back. Her errand of this afternoon had been mysterious. Melany had made very few friends during the entire three years she had been helping at the tavern. An expedition of any kind was a rare occurrence. Occasionally she ventured to one of the nearby villages to make some special purchase. Once or twice she had visited a woman who lived in Liscard, who was something of a sempstress and made gowns for her. The fact that she had returned without packages of any kind, and with the skirt of her best green silk gown bedraggled, puzzled Mother Redcap.

It had been only by pure chance that she had noticed Melany's gown.

She had been attending to customers near the doorway and so had caught a glimpse of it as the girl came in. Melany had hesitated and tried hard to conceal her mud spattered skirt and stockings, and had hastily slipped away to her room to change them before coming to help serve.

The very secretiveness of Melany's manner puzzled Mother Redcap. She felt convinced that there was a link between Melany's outing and the stranger who lay upstairs. If she had been to visit the sempstress in Liscard then it seemed likely that she would have brought back a message of some kind. Another thing, if her expedition had been so entirely blameless why did she not mention where she had been?

It was some hours before Melany was able to escape from the crowded tavern, to slip upstairs to the room where Jim Grenville lay.

He tried to pull himself up in the bed, as she drew the curtains and set down the candle she was carrying, on the table.

'Well, what luck?' he asked, eagerly; ignoring the food she was laying out for him.

'Eat some of this broth,' she instructed. 'It is a long time since you had any food, you must be feeling weak from hunger. We have been so busy that I was unable to leave my Aunt to manage on her own.'

He caught at the sleeve of her dress impatiently.

'What news have you for me?'

Then, as if reading the answer from her face, his spirits flagged, and he flopped back against his pillows.

'I might have known old Tobin would have no pity in his heart. Yet, how can I blame him. *Golden Lady* was his prize ship. To lose both her, and the treasure he knew I would have aboard, is a blow to make any man bitter.

'It was a sorry night for me, the night I sailed up the Mersey. If only my desire to set foot in Liverpool, and to see Corrina, had not been so great, I might even now have been a hero in his eyes — and hers. As it is, it would have been better if the wreckers had finished me off . . . '

'Hush!' Melany held a warning hand over his mouth. 'Keep your voice low and have a care what you say.'

Briskly she re-arranged his pillows, so that he was propped high in the bed; then placing the broth before him said, severely, 'Now, while you eat I will give you the true version of what happened this afternoon. You will find it somewhat different from the tale you have imagined I should bring you.'

It seemed for a moment that he would protest, then, recognising the authority behind her calmness, he gave in with a grin.

'Very well, I'll eat while you talk, but don't spare my feelings. If Cornelius Tobin cursed me for the fool I have been, tell me all.'

'In the first place I didn't see

Cornelius Tobin. There was a sale of black slaves, and he was among the buyers. I was unable to find him.'

Grenville stopped eating and stared at her in amazement.

'You mean you went through the streets looking for him?'

'But of course. I had promised you I would find him and give him your message. Well, I was unable to find him, as the crowds were so dense, but I did see his daughter.'

'You saw Corrina!'

Melany nodded.

'You recognised her from my description?' Grenville's voice throbbed with love and pride.

'Well, not exactly. You see when I first reached Liverpool I went straight to Cornelius Tobin's house, as you had asked me to do. While I was standing in the carriage-way, wondering which door to knock at, a gentleman approached on horseback. He enquired if he could help me. When I told him I was seeking an interview with Cornelius Tobin he told me I should find him inspecting the slaves, that were for sale, at the Goree Piazas. While I was there looking for him a carriage drew alongside me, and this same gentleman leaned from the window. He wanted to know if I had had any success in my quest. The other occupant of the carriage was a lady — yes!' she smiled as Grenville's grey eyes widened, 'it was Corrina.'

'How was she looking? Did you tell her where I was? Did you tell her that as soon as I was well enough, I should call on her? Did she send any message? Did . . . ' he pulled himself up. 'I'm sorry, Melany, I've interrupted your tale. Please go on and tell it in your own way.'

Melany smiled patiently. 'When she learned that I was looking for her father she explained who she was. I took it upon myself to tell her that I also had a message for her. I then told her how the wreckers had lured the *Golden Lady* ashore, and how all the crew had been killed. I told her how you had been washed ashore, after being badly injured. I explained how you had stumbled as far as our tavern and that we were nursing you back to health.'

'Well?'

'She seemed distressed to hear about your misfortune. She said that her father was grievously annoyed over the loss of his ship. For the present, while the matter still rankled so freshly in his mind, she thought it would be wiser if you lay low.'

'But that means not seeing *her*!'

'It is no doubt the double loss of the ship, and the treasure you carried aboard, which has upset Cornelius Tobin so much.'

Grenville nodded sadly. His whole world seemed to be crumbling round him. The loss of his ship, the loss of his treasure, the loss of Cornelius Tobin's trust, and now the thought that although he was so near to Corrina he could not meet her.

He was mortified by Corrina's

response to the news that he was alive and so near to her. He had thought that once she knew nothing could have kept them apart. All the afternoon, whilst he had feigned sleep, he had strained his ears listening for the sound of horses' hooves, or a carriage drawing up. He had felt sure that once Melany told Tobin or Corrina of his whereabouts nothing would stop her from rushing to his side. With Corrina on his side he had felt sure he would win over her father.

He had never — even at his greatest moments of despair — expected her to send back a message that he was to 'lie low'.

Wearily, he pushed the half eaten broth to one side.

'This gentleman whom you met outside Tobin's house, and who was later in the carriage with Corrina, who was he?'

For a brief second Melany hesitated, wondering whether it might be better for his peace of mind if he did not know. Under Grenville's penetrating stare her mind became confused.

'It was Lord Pendleton,' she said at last.

It seemed as if Jim Grenville's cup of bitterness overflowed. With a groan, he half turned, and buried his head in the pillows. The fact that she had been out riding with Lord Pendleton hurt his pride even more than the disinterested message regarding his welfare. All Liverpool knew Pendleton to be a weak-willed fop. Could Corrina be ogling for a title. The thought sickened him. And yet, there must surely be some understanding between them for her to be driving unchaperoned with him through the streets of Liverpool.

Picking up the half eaten broth, and the candle, Melany quietly left the room, shutting the door noiselessly behind her. There was no consolation she could offer.

She would return later, she decided, with some rum and milk and settle Grenville for the night. Then she must prime him with the story he was to tell her Aunt. They couldn't go on saying he was too weak to talk. In the meantime, she must leave him alone to fight out the battle she knew to be raging within him.

5

Ten days later Jim Grenville was ready to make his appearance downstairs. He had been getting up each day, for almost a week, and was now quite strong, and felt the need of company, other than that of Melany and her Aunt. Lying upstairs, brooding over his misfortunes, was making him depressed.

Melany had warned him to keep a close guard on his tongue when her Aunt was around. He had told Mother Redcap that he was hiding from the Press Gang and that he had received his injuries escaping from them. He told her he was a woollen journeyman from Yorkshire but that his wares, credentials, and all his money, had been taken from him by the Press Gang. He now feared his employers would consider him a thief, and a vagrant. He promised that as soon as he was strong enough he would obtain work of some kind, and repay her hospitality.

Shrewd old Cheshire woman though she was, Mother Redcap was completely fooled by his story. Not only did she agree he should stay, but also promised to help him to find work of some kind.

'There's little enough for the likes of you to do in a place like this,' she told him, 'unless you turn your hand to a bit of sea fishing. I'll warrant you know nothing at all about such things.'

'No! Nor have I very much inclination to learn about anything to do with the sea, after the treatment I got at the hands of the Press Gang,' he replied drily. 'If I could lay hold of any of those rascals, by God! I'd murder them. I'd wring the breath out of their scrawny necks with my bare hands.'

'I don't know about helping you to revenge yourself on the Press Gang, but I might be able to help you settle your odds with the Customs fellows.' Her round, rosy cheeks creased in a knowing smile, 'they're all tarred with the same brush, I'm thinking.'

'I'll accept your judgment in the matter, Mother Redcap,' Grenville replied solemnly.

Melany was apprehensive when Grenville told her of Mother Redcap's promises. She suspected that her Aunt intended to introduce him to Matt and his gang. Although she had no real proof, she suspected that they were the ones who had wrecked the *Golden Lady*. If this was so, then either Matt, or one of his men, might recognise him. Hesitantly she tried to warn him.

'There is something worrying me, something I think you should know before you go downstairs tonight.'

Jim patted the window seat beside him, invitingly. 'Come on then, sit down and tell me what it is. Are you still afraid that I may give myself away by something I might say, or do.'

'Partly that,' she agreed frankly. 'But

that's not the only thing I fear.'

He waited while she debated with herself whether to go on with her confidence.

At length she said, 'You remember the night you came here, the night the *Golden Lady* was wrecked?' She watched the pain cross his face at the memory, and she knew then that she was doing right to tell him of her fears.

'Well?' he asked impatiently.

'That night, before you came, but after we were really closed for the night, there was a great deal of activity going on downstairs. I was supposed to be abed and asleep, but the noise was so great, it disturbed me. I crept along the landing and half way down the stairs — to a place where I could see into the South Room. It was full of men and they were all drinking, and talking excitedly. They were wreckers, just back from a job.

'You mean they were the wreckers who had lured the *Golden Lady* ashore, and then ransacked her, don't you?'

She nodded.

'Do you mean to tell me that you have known all the time who they were!' A vein throbbed angrily at his temple. 'Knowing how much I've wanted to find those men, wanted my revenge, you've kept this from me and played me along like the poor fish you must take me to be. Saying nothing! Letting me lie here worrying my guts out, and thinking that I had your sympathy, while all the time you knew exactly where these men were, and who they were. Good God! Does it mean that not five minutes after you'd been spooning some of your soothing syrup down my throat you were back downstairs laughing and chaffing with the very men who lured me onto this damn beach? The very men who plundered the *Golden Lady* and stole the treasure I had on board. The men who massacred my crew; the men who left me . . . '

'Hush! Please hush!' She laid a restraining hand on his arm. 'Don't raise your voice like that or my Aunt will hear you. At all costs she must not know who you are. What you say may have some truth in it. My job here is to serve my Aunt's customers, not to question who they are, or how they make a living. Remember, I did all I could to help you. I went to Liverpool — not a very successful venture I grant you, but that was hardly my fault! My Aunt thinks that the night the wreckers came here I was in bed and asleep. She has never told me of their activities. Nor for that matter does she ever discuss with me the queer goings-on in and around this house. The entire place is riddled with hiding places, secret passages, and tunnels. I know of course that she hides loot for sailors who are escaping from the law, or dodging the Customs men. I know she often plays her part in the smuggling that goes on around the coast. Many a time I have set the weather vane to warn some sailor who is expected that there are Customs men about, and he is to keep away. Such everyday affairs, though secret in some respects, are commonplace enough. But the bigger things, like wrecking, or murder, she keeps to herself and those directly concerned.'

She paused, and looked at Jim Grenville but his face was as set as if it had been carved from a granite slab.

She went on, 'I felt I should warn you because I think my Aunt intends to introduce you to Matt and his gang. She appears to believe your story that you were the victim of the Press Gang and may be doing it because she thinks you may be of use to Matt. Or it may be that she half suspects you are from the *Golden Lady* and it may be a trap she has planned with Matt. I just wanted you to be on your guard. Above all, if you do recognise him or any of his men as being your attackers, don't lose control of your feelings. Remember, you are still a sick man. If they thought there was any chance of you betraying them they would not think twice about killing you. They are callous brutes and have no respect for the law.'

There was a long silence when she had finished, then awkwardly Grenville put his hand on her arm.

'I'm sorry, Melany, for my harsh words, and for doubting you. I'll be careful of what I say, and do, for both our sakes. Someday I'll repay you for all your kindness to me. At the moment, all I can think of is revenge. These men have wrecked my hopes and dreams and put me in the position I am in now. If what you think is true, and through your Aunt I come face to face with this fellow Matt, then fate is indeed playing into my hands.' His grey eyes shone with renewed hope. 'If I can win their confidence, and prove that they were responsible for the dastardly crime, I might also discover the whereabouts of the treasure they stole from my cabin. Who knows, I may even recover it!

With that once more in my possession I could face Cornelius Tobin without flinching. He would soon forgive the loss of the *Golden Lady* if he had that to compensate him.' He rose from the seat and began to pace up and down the small room.

'There is only one man I would be likely to recognise, that would be the fellow who knocked me out. I think I might know him again, tho' it all happened so quickly. If he should show signs of recognising me,' he said hastily seeing the fear in her eyes, 'I will be able to handle the situation all right, and not give myself away.'

'Melany,' his arm slid round her slim shoulders, and with his other hand he tilted her face, until his grey eyes were looking deep into her brown ones. 'Melany,' he murmured again softly, 'forgive me for the way I spoke to you just now.'

A wonderful sensation filled her at his touch. She nodded, too disturbed to speak. Gently, almost reverently, he bent his head until their lips met. Then hungrily he pulled her into his arms, crushing her against his lean body. He kissed her with a burning passion that almost choked her. It sent the blood pounding to her head, made her ears sing. She felt her heart beat wildly as if it would break the imprisonment of her body and burst with the intoxicating joy, and love, that filled it. Timidly, at first, she returned his embrace, and then her ardour grew until it was as burning and passionate as his own. Her arms were round his neck. As he held her even closer to him, her body strained against his.

He was the first man who had awakened her emotions, and her love burned the fiercer because of it. When at length he gently released her she felt limp, but pleasurably elated. Her eyes, as they opened and looked into his, were like two great dark stars, yet soft as velvet, brimming over with love for him.

Kissing her gently on the brow he murmured, 'For both our sakes I'll be careful, Melany.'

Leaving her abruptly he went swiftly down the stairs to the tavern.

6

Melany served ale to the crowded room in a dreamy daze, hearing none of the chaffing that went on all around her. Her eyes were only for one man in the room, the man to whom she had utterly, and completely, lost her heart.

Yet to what purpose. Despite his present set-back she felt sure he would not be content until he had cleared himself in the eyes of both Corrina and Cornelius Tobin. Her love, she feared, could never hope to erase from his mind the picture he carried of Corrina.

Resolutely Melany determined not to dwell on the matter. She was being foolish to attach too much importance to the fact that he had taken her into his arms and awakened a passion in her she had never known before. It possibly meant little enough to him.

Yet, though she told herself these things, her subconscious mind revelled in much sweeter thoughts. If he had merely been expressing gratitude for her help then his passion would have been much more controlled. She knew he had been at sea for many months and deprived of women's company but surely he was not the sort of man to stir a girl's heart unless his feelings went deeply. She shivered at the memory of his tender touch, his burning kisses, the feeling of unity that had engulfed her when his arms had enfolded her.

She watched him across the crowded room. It was easy to follow his movements. He was head and shoulders taller than most of the men gathered there. His shock of red hair burned like a fiery torch among the dark swarthy heads and drab knitted caps of the general crowd. His pallor contrasted noticeably to their tanned and swarthy faces, and he appeared thin, almost emaciated. He was wearing clothes she had bought from a widow living at Poulton whose husband had been drowned, only a few weeks earlier.

She wished her Aunt had not taken it into her head to try and find him work especially with Matt, since she was sure he had led the men who had wrecked the *Golden Lady*. For Grenville to mix with them was asking for trouble. There was no knowing what would happen if Matt suspected Grenville's true identity. Matt's temper was short and he was ruthless and brutal when provoked.

Her sense of foreboding increased when Sammy moved to her side and said urgently, 'I must speak with you. Come outside. Be by the well in five minutes.'

She continued to serve as if nothing had happened, then, as she noticed him rise from his seat and sidle towards the back door, she followed him.

Sammy was waiting in the shadows as she joined him and he motioned her to be quiet.

'That fellow, that red-headed one,

who's with Matt tonight, who is he?'

For a moment she hesitated, trying to think what to say and wondering why he asked. Sammy's next words startled her.

'He's from the *Golden Lady*. Don't lie to me. God! I'll never forget his face. It's haunted me every hour of the night and day since the night of the wreck.'

She loosened Sammy's hand from her arm, which felt bruised under his fingers.

'You're hurting me,' she protested.

'For God's sake tell me who that fellow is, and how he comes to be with Matt tonight.'

'My Aunt introduced him to Matt.'

'You're not helping me, Melany.' He ran his hand through his thick straight hair until it stood on end, wiry and unkempt.

'Melany.' He took her arm again, his voice was hoarse as he pleaded. 'You must try to understand. I've got to know who he is. Both his life, and mine, may be in danger if he's the man I take him to be.'

Melany desperately played for time. 'Who do you think he is?'

With a groan, Sammy took his hand from her arm and passed it over his eyes. 'Have you forgotten, Melany, the night the *Golden Lady* was wrecked I was one of Matt's gang.'

She shook her head. 'No, how could I.'

He went on as if he had not heard her. 'I told you about my first night with them . . . on a job that is. Matt gave the instructions when he saw the boat heading fast towards our coast. We were to wait until the boat beached then, as the men aboard her jumped over the side, we were to club them down while they were still shocked from the coldness of the sea.'

He paused and the scene Sammy was re-living came vividly to Melany. The bare beach, the glistening eddying waters and the great ship keeled over in the shallow water. Then as men jumped and scrambled from her, in an effort to save their lives, how they were battered insensible by Matt and his men, who lay there waiting for them.

Sammy went on, 'It all happened so suddenly that I forgot all the instructions Matt had given me. I stood there, watching the ghastly work that Matt and his men were doing.'

A shudder went through him at the memory.

'Then Matt missed me. He turned to look for me and saw me well back on the dunes; just watching and doing nothing to help them. He called to me to come and do my share. At that moment, a man ran past him, heading inland. He called out to me to stop him.

'Use your club,' he yelled. Knowing he was watching me, I lashed out with my wooden club as the fellow drew alongside me. My aim was pretty wild. The club only grazed the man's head. He had courage. He cursed me for the fool I was, and threatened what would happen to us all.

That's when I must have lost my head. Like a mad-man I swung the club again, and the fellow lay unconscious at my feet.

He was very tall, and as he fell the moonlight shone on his face and head. He had red hair. I didn't stop to make sure he was dead. He was lying almost completely under water and there wasn't a movement from him. His face and head were streaming with blood. I felt sick. All I wanted to do was to put as much of the shore between his body and me as I could. The sight of his white, lifeless face, shining like a ghostie in the moonlight, sent chills through me. My teeth chattered as I stumbled along to where Matt and the rest were. Even their company was good after that.'

'Why are you telling me all this, Sammy?'

'Tonight I've seen that same face, the same red hair. That man who is in there talking to Matt is the man I thought I'd killed!'

A cold horror spread through Melany. She felt numb with despair. If Sammy told Matt of his fears, and they proved to be right, Matt would have no hesitation in killing Grenville, just to silence him.

She looked at Sammy. His face was white and his lips trembling. At all costs Sammy must be silenced. He must be made to forget his suspicions. Jim must be warned.

Affecting a laugh, she patted his arm.

'You know your trouble, Sammy, you need a good strong drink. Come back inside, and I'll see you get a glass of my Aunt's homebrewed; and what's more, I'll lace it good and strong with some of the best rum you've ever tasted.'

As he tried to interrupt she slipped her arm through his.

'Fancy thinking that a man you clubbed and left lying in the sea could possibly be still alive. The trouble is you've got this clubbing business on your mind and you're haunted. If you don't watch yourself you'll imagine that every red-headed man you meet is the man you killed; or his ghost come back to haunt you.'

'He's no ghost,' muttered Sammy. 'He's real enough. He's in that room,' he jerked a thumb in the direction of the tavern, 'drinking and eating.'

'Of course that red-headed fellow in there is real enough,' laughed Melany. 'He's trying to avoid the Press Gang, that's why he's here. He's hiding. My Aunt wants Matt to help him, only it's supposed to be a secret, so don't go blabbing it to anyone.'

Sammy looked a little easier. 'You're sure of that, Melany? You're not just saying that to please me, to make me easier in my mind?'

'You can ask my Aunt if you don't believe me,' she said coldly, taking her hand from his arm.

'Don't go, Melany.' He caught at

her dress. 'It's not that I don't believe you. I feel so scared at meeting that man again that I can't think properly. I didn't mean to say anything to upset you.'

She relented, and patted his arm consolingly.

'Now do stop worrying, Sammy. The man you clubbed could hardly be sitting drinking ale. Just look at your muscles and you'll know I'm telling the truth. One blow from your club would fell a man, and no mistake.'

Sammy grinned, boyishly. 'You think so. You think I'm as good as Matt and his crowd?'

'You're stronger than any of them but what good is that if you're going to worry yourself sick every time you go on a job with them. They don't worry about it afterwards, I can tell you. You want to forget all about that night, and enjoy the spoils — I'll bet there were plenty.'

Sammy grinned again. 'We haven't had the share-out yet, but Matt promises plenty. I'm looking forward to that I can tell you. I'm glad I told you about my fears, Melany. Strange thing is I feel much better about it now. You know, I think perhaps you're right, that fellow is like the man I clubbed that night, and yet he isn't. Must be because they both had red hair. The fellow I clubbed was much bigger than this chap. He was a massive man. I remember looking down at him, as he lay there at my feet, and marvelling as to how I had managed to knock him out.'

Melany slipped her slim hand into Sammy's large broad one and gave it a friendly squeeze. 'How about us going inside again, and I'll get that drink I promised you. Let me go first, before my Aunt misses me.'

'Thanks, Melany, you've been a good friend, letting me talk. I . . . I'll remember you when Matt shares out.'

Melany slipped away. She hoped no one had noticed her absence. She felt relieved that she had convinced Sammy that he had been mistaken about Grenville. At all costs Matt's suspicions mustn't be aroused.

The bar was noisy and crowded. As soon as Sammy came in she passed him his drink and said in a low voice: 'Drink to our secret! My, how Matt would ridicule you if he knew what you had told me tonight.'

Sammy flushed. 'I know,' he said, in a shamefaced manner. 'You won't let on to him, will you? I've had another look at that fellow, and I can't for the life of me think how I came to even imagine that he was the man I had clubbed.'

Melany smiled up at him. 'Never mind, Sammy. I'll keep your secret. I'm glad you told me. It makes you different somehow from the others.'

His face brightened. 'You mean that, Melany?' He grasped eagerly at the thread of hope she so tentatively offered. 'Will you let me see you sometimes . . . alone.'

'You can ask, Sammy, but I'm not making any promises.'

'Please try, Melany.'

She smiled at his eagerness: 'Very well,' she answered, non-commitally.

7

Jim Grenville was elated by his meeting with Matt. Early the next morning, he sought Melany out. He found her in the yard behind the tavern feeding the hens. Taking her firmly by the hand he began to lead her towards the foreshore where he could tell her all about it without fear of being overheard.

'But Jim,' she protested, 'I must help my Aunt. The rooms have to be cleaned, and the meals prepared, before we begin to get busy.'

'Nonsense! You can spare half an hour. Look how the sun is shining, urging you to come out. If you listen to the tide you'll hear it whispering the promise of a glorious day. Look, even the gulls are swooping low, saying 'good-morning' to you in their own fashion.'

Melany laughed. 'You are in a poetic mood. You must be feeling better.'

He waved an arm expressively, embracing the richness of the morning that was displayed around them. 'Who could help but feel well and enjoy being alive,' he exclaimed.

To their right lay the sea, blue and sparkling, licking the edge of the sand and shingle leaving them glistening in the sunlight as though strewn with precious stones. To their left the sand dunes rose like sentinels, a natural barrier between water and land. Their tops were green with the short coarse grass that seemed to flourish on the sandy soil. Farther inland as far as the eye could see were the motley greens of moss and moor. Bidston Hill rose suddenly like a backcloth. Behind that again were the dim bluish-grey outlines of the Welsh mountains.

Most times the scene was a bleak and desolate one, but this morning early sunshine cast a magical spell. Even the grey stone cottages, clustered away to the west at Liscard and to the north at Wallasey fitted harmoniously into the general picture. Snuggling into hollows they blended with the landscape, and only thin wisps of smoke from their stubby chimneys showed that human life was present.

Only two buildings stood out against the skyline. High on a hill midway between the two villages stood the Church of St. Hilary, grey and gaunt, while on the north eastern ridge there was a lighthouse. Apart from these the skyline was barren as far as the look-out tower on the highest point of Bidston Hill.

Jim Grenville glanced down at the girl at his side with pleasure. She wore a peony red homespun gown, its wide skirt nipped in tightly at the waist, the embroidered bodice buttoned to the neck. Her dark hair was caught back from her face and the wind whipped tiny tendrils into a froth of minute curls around her ears and temples. Her cheeks glowed, her eyes shone, and her lips were parted in a half smile of happiness.

He saw her look of delight fade as he related to her the conversation he had had with Matt the previous night. She waited until he had finished then laid a hand on his arm. 'Let me ask you something,' she said quietly. 'Did you notice a youngish fellow with Matt and his crowd? A tall lad, just on twenty, rather gangling, with a beardless face and a soft voice.'

Jim shook his head. 'Does it matter?'

'I wish you had seen him. He sought me out during the evening. He was in a fine state of fear. On the night of the wreck he had been one of Matt's gang. He was the chap who clubbed you. He hasn't been able to put the matter out of his mind since the night it happened. Seeing you again — risen up as if from the dead — and to find you actually talking to Matt, really scared him.'

Jim's face grew white as he listened to Melany. His eyes became grey slits. 'And what does he propose to do?' he asked in clipped tones.

'For the moment nothing. I convinced him he was mistaken and that you had escaped from the Press Gang, and that my Aunt was giving you shelter. He eventually agreed that it was only your red hair that made him think you were the man he had clubbed.'

Grenville let out a long sigh of relief as he squeezed her arm appreciatively. 'You're my guardian angel, Melany, and no mistake. Did you learn anything else?'

'Well, it's proof that it was Matt and his gang who wrecked the *Golden Lady*. Another thing I learned from Sammy was that they haven't had their share-out yet.'

'Oh!' Jim looked down at her with quickened interest. 'How can you be sure?'

She blushed slightly as she told him: 'Sammy has promised to give me a day out, or to buy me a keep-sake, when they do.'

'You little flirt,' laughed Jim. 'I bet

before they have the share-out you'll get a promise from all of them to do the same thing.'

Melany bit her lip to keep back the sudden stinging tears that flooded her eyes. The last thing she wanted Jim to think was that she was a girl who would smile at any man in order to extract a confidence. She regretted having told him of Sammy's promise. Couldn't he understand that she had done it only because of her feelings for him.

Noticing her silence Jim stopped and raised her face to his. The sight of her brown eyes bright with tears filled him with quick remorse for his thoughtlessness.

'Melany,' he said softly, 'I know you did it for me. I was only jesting when I said what I did. Will you forgive me?'

His grey eyes pleaded as they looked into hers. She nodded, not trusting herself to speak. A longing to run her fingers through his fiery auburn hair seized her so strongly that she clenched her hands together to resist the urge.

Gently he bent and kissed her lips. Not the burning passionate kiss of the night before, not the kiss of a man hungry for the taste of a woman's lips, but the kiss of a man whose heart was overflowing with love and gratitude. A long tender kiss that made the tears, so near to spilling, trickle through her closed lids and down her cheeks.

'Don't cry my darling.' Gently he dried her eyes. 'Look at me. Tell me I've not upset you. Tell me you'll still help me.'

The response in her large dark eyes told him clearer than any words of the love and sweetness she would give without hesitation. They revealed how none, but he, could subdue the new found feelings, so recently awakened in her mind and heart.

The wonder of it disturbed him. Melany was no ordinary country girl whom he could kiss and leave; with whom he could pass a pleasant hour and then forget.

Unbidden, a vision of Corrina,

her golden hair framing the perfect regularity of her features, blotted Melany from his thoughts. He saw again the vivid blue eyes, that had looked up at him so adoringly as they had taken their leave of each other on the quayside, before he had set off in the *Golden Lady* on his ill fated voyage. He could almost smell the headiness of the perfume she always used and hear the rustle of her rich gown.

He passed a hand over his eyes, as if to brush away the vision. Corrina and her father belonged to the past. To all intents and purposes he might as well be dead, as far as they were concerned.

Melany, seeing him sway, was contritely aware that he was still a sick man.

'Oh, Jim!' she exclaimed filled with concern. 'I've let you walk too far and exert yourself. I quite forgot that this was the first time you had been out of doors. If you feel faint we'll sit down for a while and rest.'

Jim smiled into the sweet face that

was so anxiously looking up at him. Gently he stroked her dark hair that the breeze had stirred into a halo round her small face.

'You go back to the tavern. I'll rest here for a while. I have so much to think about and plan for the future. I'll be able to think more clearly in the open. You go on back to the tavern, and I'll rest here for a while.'

She nodded understandingly. 'Very well, but be careful.'

'Careful?'

'About what you think. Don't plan anything rash. Far better that you start life anew. You could always use another name and join a ship from Liverpool. Don't risk your life just to outwit Matt. He's twice your years; and his cunning is many times greater than yours could ever be. He's evil! I've heard men mutter about him when they've been drunk, and when they've been sober. Many have threatened revenge but none have ever succeeded. Please be careful, Jim. If anything should happen to you . . . ' she hesitated, her voice choking, as she found it too difficult to finish.

Without a backward glance she began to run quickly over the shingle — back to Mother Redcap's.

Jim Grenville watched her until she became just a moving dot on the bright, sunlit beach.

8

Jim's chance to earn Matt's confidence came sooner than either he, or Melany, had anticipated. Less than a week after their first meeting Matt approached him.

'The job's dangerous,' warned Matt. 'If you get caught I want no part in it. And, remember, no one squeals twice on me. Before anyone can help you they'll find you with your throat slit from ear to ear. Mark my words! You have to be tough to work for me. The work is dangerous. Prove yourself and the rewards will be well worth the risks you take.'

'I'm not scared,' Jim replied quietly. 'Neither do I squeal. I learned my lessons in life the hard way, and I know how to keep my own counsel.'

Matt looked at him shrewdly. 'I'm taking a deal of a risk with you. There's devil of a little you've given away about yourself. For all I know you may be a spy for the Preventive Officers from Liverpool.'

Jim laughed scornfully, and indicated his clothes. 'Do you think I'd be garbed like this if I was. Don't you know these clothes when you see them? They belonged to a fisherman from Poulton who was drowned a couple of weeks ago. Melany bought them from the man's wife for me. As yet I haven't even paid for them.'

'You might be wearing them as a disguise.'

Jim laughed contemptuously. 'Mother Redcap will vouch for me. Heaven knows she should recognise a Preventive Officer when she meets up with one, disguise or no disguise.'

'All the same,' Matt argued, 'all I've been told, and that by Mother Redcap, not by you, is that you're hiding out from the Press Gang. She says you were injured so she gave you shelter, and nursed you back to health.'

'She didn't do any of the nursing, her niece Melany did that — and a rare fine job she made of it,' Grenville said quietly.

'Just so. But what else? Who are you really, and where did you come from before the Press Gang laid hands on you? You're not from this side of the water.'

Jim smiled. 'There's many a mile of land on the other side of the Mersey.'

'So you won't speak any further, eh?' Matt's mouth was a hard line and his green eyes cold and brittle as he measured Jim up.

Grenville met his gaze steadily. 'I've already told you I've learned, the hard way, that it's wiser to keep my own counsel. I don't gossip about other people's secrets, neither do I blab about my own. If you can't take me at my face value, and from what Mother Redcap has told me . . . ' he shrugged expressively . . . 'I'll be looking around for other ways of earning my keep.'

'Not so fast. I like a man who

can keep his mouth shut. You and I should get along together fine. That's if you can act as quickly and silently as you live.'

'I know my way around. Tell me what you want me to do. I'll ask no questions, providing it is made worth my while.'

For the first time Matt smiled. Clasping Jim by the arm he led him to a window seat, and thumped loudly on the small table nearby.

'Sit down. We'll drink on this. Drink to our new venture and to success.' The smile faded for a moment, leaving his face hard as granite and his eyes steely cold. 'Let's understand one another right now. We'll drink to success because I can't stand failures. Understand. No man fails me twice. I expect men to take orders and carry them out with no questions asked. I'll tell you just as much as I want you to know. If you guess more, then that's your affair; but I don't want it to reach my ears. I like a man who can work swiftly, and quietly, and without any kind of fuss. I'm a hard man, Grenville. To wrest a living in these times you have to be. Everything is against us. Nature. The law. The position of the land itself. The only thing this God forsaken waste is any good for is smuggling and wrecking. The land is too barren and bleak to farm, crops wither and cattle starve. When the sea turns against us it is flood and marsh. Every hamlet round here is peopled by smugglers, and wreckers; law breakers of one kind or another. Even the parson will stop in the middle of his sermon, and desert the pulpit, if the news of a wreck reaches him.

But enough of this. You have eyes in your head, ears as well, and by now this should be obvious to you. Whatever place you come from it must be pretty poor that you prefer to stay here instead of returning to it. Or else, you have left some smudge behind you that it is easier to let time erase, than try to right yourself. If you won't talk about it then I'll let the matter drop.'

He raised his voice. 'Bring on some ale, and a plate of your ham and eggs, Mother Redcap. We would sample both, but be quick with the ale.'

As Jim raised his tankard to pledge his allegiance, he felt a shiver of apprehension run through him. Melany's warning came back to him.

His voice was a trifle strained, as he said, 'To our venture. To a long life, and a prosperous one.'

Raising his tankard, Matt nodded, and drained the full measure at one swift drink.

With a great effort Jim did the same.

The pint of cold ale almost benumbed him. It stabbed his throat like an icy dagger. It took all his will power to keep the tankard at his lips and go on swallowing.

He knew Matt was watching him.

He took longer than Matt to complete the feat, but when he set down his tankard it was empty.

Matt seemed to relax; 'Now here is the plan. Listen carefully. At midnight, just when the tide is on the turn, a small boat will pull into 'Red Bett's Pool' just below the house here, where the stream runs into the sea — you know it?'

Jim nodded.

'To the left of the pool there's a cave opening. You will hide there until the men in the boat signal. They will hand you a bundle. Wait in the cave until they pull away then, if everything is safe, you can leave right away with the package. It's to be delivered to the Ring o' Bells at Bidston. Is that clear?'

Jim nodded, then asked, 'Do I take any particular route?'

Matts' eyes narrowed. 'There is only one way when you're smuggling contraband.'

'You'll leave by a tunnel which has an entrance beside the well in the backyard. It runs for about three hundred yards uphill. Suddenly you'll come to ground surface, in a sort of pit. There's shrubs overhanging so you are safe from sight. From this point there's a clear view of the river and the moor. Go straight across the moor, skirting the village at Liscard, but picking up the footpath again over the Moss. Watch your step, the moor is treacherous, but if you follow the footpath you will come to the Jawbones. You've heard of them?'

Jim shook his head.

Matt looked grim. 'Well, 'tis a kind of bridge over the worst of the pools, formed by the jawbones of a whale that was washed up on these shores many years ago. Folks do say as how the ghosts of men who stumbled to their death when crossing there haunt the place. If you're scared of ghosts and such . . . ' he left the sentence unfinished.

Jim's jaw instinctively jutted. 'I'm not afraid of anything living, nor dead; nor anything that hovers between the two, if such beings exist.'

His eyes met Matt's and held them in a long stare.

'Glad to hear it,' Matt commented. 'You'll need all your courage and keep your wits sharp. The Moss is no easy place on a dark night, even when you know it. From the Jawbones follow the track to the South and it will lead you right to the Ring o' Bells. Tap twice on the back door. When the Landlord answers say to him; 'I'll have a tankard of Mother Redcap's best home-brewed ale, well laced.' He'll then ask you inside and your job is over. Hand him the package, rest there until daylight, and then return by any route you please. Tomorrow night, if I hear your mission has been successful, I will see you here and pay you for your trouble.'

'It seems simple enough, where is the danger?'

Matt laughed: 'You have a suspicious nature.'

Jim shrugged. 'Merely curious as to why you should hand me such a plum job. You must have a dozen men who could do it better than I; who know the path from here to the Ring o' Bells blindfold.'

For a moment Matt looked angry. 'I'll not be questioned and badgered, by the men I use,' he snapped. Then his face relaxed; 'You were not to know that. My reasons are simple enough.'

'Well,' Jim waited for his explanation.

'The package you'll carry is tobacco. A ship was wrecked two nights back, on Wallasey beach, but the tobacco has been hidden in a cave nearby. The Preventive Officers know about the wreck, by now, and they'll also know that some of the cargo is missing, so they'll be on the look out. Most of my men are too well known to them to smuggle it to the Ring o' Bells, so I'm using you.' He laughed harshly. 'Do this job well and a great future in smuggling might be yours. Fail and . . . ' he shrugged and left the sentence unfinished.

Jim nodded. 'And by failing you

mean let the Preventive Officers catch me.'

Matt shook his head. 'I'll see that you don't get caught by the Preventive Officers. The Moss is your real hazard. Some it befriends and for them it opens up its paths willingly.'

'In other words, Matt, if I master the bog I'm in with your gang; if the bog masters me, well . . . that's the end of the story.'

'I've always found the bog to be a true judge of men,' Matt replied evasively.

'And in the meantime you and your men entertain the Preventive Officers here at Mother Redcaps?'

'Something like that. You'll be safe from them.'

Jim rose to his feet. 'The deal's on.'

9

Emerging from the cave behind Mother Redcap's, Jim Grenville looked carefully round him. The bundle he carried was quite large and he judged it to hold some ten or twelve pounds of tobacco. It was stoutly wrapped and tied. Probably to prevent me pinching any, thought Jim, grimly. He had no illusions as to how far Matt trusted him.

The plans, as laid down by Matt, had so far been easy to follow, but he felt rather dubious as to the outcome of his journey. When he had told Melany about the proposed scheme she had been aghast at the thought of him attempting to cross the Moss by night. It was a treacherous labyrinth of pools, and morasses, she warned him, and even those who knew it well, would not attempt to cross it after dark.

Jim waved aside her fears. Surely if he could chart unknown seas, which were thousands of miles wide, it should not be difficult to find his way across three miles of marshy ground.

She told him tales of men who had set out to cross the Moss on dark nights and had never been seen again, nor for that matter were their bodies ever found. She told him of the legend of the Jawbones, and how it was reputed to be haunted.

Although there was no moon the night was clear, and as he drew near to Liscard he could make out the shapes of the huddle of cottages that made up the village. Remembering Matt's instructions he left the roadway and took a devious route, keeping out of sight close to the hedges and then picked up the road again about a mile or so further on.

Almost immediately the land began to drop towards the Moss, and very soon the road had become just a narrow, twisting, overgrown pathway.

As he followed it he felt as if he were walking into a curtain of mist. Twice he stepped off the pathway and felt his feet slowly sinking in the marshy ground that flanked it.

Melany had not been speaking idly when she had warned him of the dangerous treachery of the Moss. He stopped and tried to think out his best method of approach. The bundle he was carrying was already beginning to feel heavy. He wished he had a length of rope so that he could have secured the bundle to his back, and left his hands free to help guide him through the darkness. His feet were soaking wet from the marshy land. As the mist thickened he seemed to be in a world apart, cut off from everywhere, a place where there was neither sight nor sound. Living creatures of every sort, seemed to have deserted the Moss. There was not even the rustle of a mouse in the dank grass.

A dread that he might never reach the Ring o' Bells suddenly filled Grenville.

He cursed himself for being foolish enough to have taken on Matt's assignment without having first seen the Moss in daylight. To try and cross such a morass in the dead of night was foolhardy, and yet it was important that he became one of Matt's gang at the earliest opportunity. It was the only way he would discover the whereabouts of the treasure that Matt had looted from the *Golden Lady*, before it was disposed of by the gang.

Taking a firm grip on himself Jim once more set off. He had barely taken a dozen steps forward when once again he felt the ground become soft beneath his feet and heard the squelch of water through his boots.

Cursing, he retraced his steps until he could feel the hard rough stones of the path. Then, step by step, he edged his way forward, through the damp mist that now blotted out everything from his sight. He walked for what must have been another mile. To him it seemed eternity. The mist chilled him to the bone. His hands were numb with holding the parcel, and his feet were icy, sodden weights, which grew heavier with every step. Although chilled through he dare not hurry since each fresh step had to be tested before putting his full weight on it.

Suddenly the path came to an end. All round him he could feel that the ground was soggy and miry. Only the small island where he stood seemed to be firm. He lowered his bundle, placing it between his feet, and bending down felt with his hands over the ground. At first he could feel nothing but squelchy marshland; then, when he was almost despairing, he felt what seemed to be a stone of some kind. Triumph and elation filled him. This must be the Jawbones that both Melany and Matt had told him about. He laughed aloud in relief. He had not lost his way after all. Once across the Jawbones just ten minutes fast walking would bring him to the Ring o' Bells. He could already savour the tankard of ale, laced with rum, that awaited him there; and taste the tang of the Cheshire cheese, and feel the satisfying warmth of the fire.

So great was his elation that for the moment he overlooked the fact that he still had the most treacherous part of the journey to make — the crossing of the Jawbones themselves.

They were slippery and narrow, and to a man whose boots were slimy with mud, and whose feet were frozen by cold, it was no easy feat to balance on their surface and carry a large bulky parcel.

He made several false starts but it was no good. Groaning with fatigue, cold and frustrated, he sat down on the one patch of sound ground, and cursed aloud. There was nothing for it but to wait until the first silver shreds of dawn slipped through the wet, grey curtain of mist that shrouded everything. Within minutes he knew this was impractical. He was already half frozen, in another half an hour he would be beyond help. He made one last effort. Removing his boots he pulled out the laces. One lace he used to secure the two boots together. The other lace he tied round the parcel, then joining the two laces he slipped them round his neck. Although the parcel outweighed the boots, and the balance was uneven, by tilting his head to one side Jim managed to keep them steady. Cautiously, on all fours, he made his way across the Jawbones bridge. Before he had taken half a dozen steps he realised the precariousness of his position. The laces were cutting into his neck yet he dare not move his head the slightest bit to alleviate the pain in case both boots and parcel slipped into the bog. If it did, he knew only too well, that before he could reach down it would have been sucked under. A similar fate would be his if he slipped from his perilous position.

He had come too far to turn back and he had no idea how far it was to the Bidston side, and comparative safety. Clenching his teeth, in an effort to overcome the cramp, and pain, in his neck, he edged forward. Sweat poured from his forehead, and his body crawled with a chilling fear. Inch by inch he moved forward into the mist, edging himself along the slippery surface of the Jawbones. All the while he was conscious of the searing pain of the laces cutting into his neck.

At last he felt the roughness of solid ground. With a moan of relief he flung himself at it, and lay there, his aching body relaxed, utterly exhausted.

Recovering his strength he roused himself and set off towards the Ring o' Bells. The very feel of hard ground revived him. Reaching the back door of the Ring o' Bells he rapped three times and when a man appeared he gave the pre-arranged signal: 'A glass of Mother Redcap's home-brewed ale, well laced.'

To his relief the man opened the door and signalled to him to enter.

The room he was taken to was a large, square, flagged kitchen. In the fireplace glowed the embers of a dying fire. Jim made for it and drew off his wet boots and outer clothing. The man watched him in silence.

'Here,' Jim held out to him the bundle of tobacco he had carried for so many arduous miles.

The man took it with a tight lipped smile, and threw it, almost contemptuously, into a corner. The great sheepdog that had been lying motionless before the fire, sniffed it disdainfully.

'That's no way to treat precious contraband,' admonished Jim. 'I've risked my life to get that bundle safely to you.'

The man's face remained impassive.

Jim shrugged. 'I've done my part. My orders were to deliver it to you. What you do with it is your affair.'

The man's voice rang with scorn. 'And how would you have me treat a bundle of cabbage leaves?'

Jim looked at him aghast. 'A bundle of what?'

'Cabbage leaves!' The man seemed to delight in the disbelief on Jim's face. 'If you don't believe it, look for yourself. Go on! You have my permission.'

'You must be out of your mind. I've crossed the Moss, over the Jawbones themselves, to bring that bundle safely to you.'

He stared closer at the man. 'You were expecting me? Has there been some ghastly mistake. You seemed to know the signal.'

'Don't worry. I was told to expect you — if you managed to cross the Moss, and the Jawbones. The parcel is still what I said it was — a bundle of cabbage leaves. The real contraband, the tobacco you thought it contained, arrived here some two hours ago.'

'I don't believe you!' Jim burst out. Hot anger at the trick that had been played on him seared his brain. 'This is a trick on your part, to take the tobacco, and then say I never brought it.'

The man remained unmoved. 'Why don't you open the parcel, and see for yourself if I lie, or not.'

'Yes, why don't you?' echoed a familiar voice.

In disbelief, Grenville swung round to see Matt's tall, figure standing in the doorway, watching him with an amused glint in his eyes.

10

Corrina was delighted with her Blackamoor. She reclined on the pink couch in her sitting-room idly dreaming. Through half shut eyes she watched the black boy as he plied the large feather fan backwards and forwards a few yards away from her.

She straightened the folds of her powder blue satin gown, allowing the fullness to drape in graceful folds over the side of the sofa, and rest on the rich grey carpet. It would be pleasant, she mused, to see the expressions on the faces of her friends when next she visited them with the Blackamoor in attendance. Especially when they learned that he was a gift from Lord Pendleton.

Once again she thought over the events of that afternoon. A frown momentarily marred her sereneness as she recalled the dark haired girl, in the green gown, who had spoken to them, bringing news of Jim Grenville.

She had been haunted by a memory of Grenville since the night they had kissed a fond farewell before he had set out in her father's ship, the *Golden Lady*. His quest was for treasure that her father knew to be hidden on some distant, unchartered island, in the Pacific Ocean.

She pictured Jim Grenville again, in his smartly cut uniform, standing bareheaded before her, as he took his leave. She remembered the flash of his smile, the unruly glint of his auburn hair. Involuntarily she compared his bronzed, outdoor manliness with the be-powdered, be-wigged, insipid looks of Lord Pendleton.

She sighed. It seemed that one could not have a husband who was both handsome and rich. Even if Grenville had brought back the treasure, and her father had been liberal with his rewards, she would not have had the same social status as his wife as she would if she married Lord Pendleton. She suspected that he would not propose until he was assured that her father would settle a handsome wedding dowry on her. Knowing her father's ambitions for her socially, she had no doubt that he would comply suitably when the time came.

At the moment, it was pleasant to bask in Lord Pendleton's attentions and the envy of her less fortunate friends. The present of the Blackamoor was just one further instance of his intentions.

Idly she studied the boy. He was a fascinating creature of about ten years old. It amused her to see how the elegant luxury of her boudoir, with its expensive pink satin curtains and hangings, and luxurious grey carpets made a pleasing background for the boy's colouring. He would be a perfect foil for her once he was suitably dressed. His rich blackness would enhance the transparent, delicate look she contrived to convey. She ran her thin tapering fingers through her light gold hair, and gave a fluttering sigh of delight at the picture.

The clothes he had on were ill-fitting and of poor quality. They had been purchased cheaply so that he might be respectfully covered before being delivered to her. She must see about providing him with some special livery. Something conspicuous. She toyed with the idea of pale blue satin trousers, a cream coloured coat and a matching turban; immediately she changed her mind in favour of scarlet trousers and a gold jacket; or even purple and green. No, she dismissed the subject, she was much too fatigued to consider the matter seriously. She would ask Lord Pendleton's advice. Men liked to be consulted on such matters — at least, she knew Lord Pendleton would like to be. She could hardly repress a smile as she imagined Grenville's reaction to such a question. Probably he was against keeping Blackamoors at all. She remembered how once he refused a commission from her father, because the ship had been going out to Africa to collect slaves. There had been long and heated arguments which she had made no attempt to understand.

She signalled with her hand for the Blackamoor to cease his fanning and to approach.

As he did so, she said loudly, and slowly, 'What is your name?'

The youth grinned with delight, showing a set of large, white, perfectly even teeth.

'Me Nabob!'

Corrina sat more upright on her couch. 'How is it you speak and understand English?'

He smiled slowly, obviously pleased at her attention, but as if not understanding.

Speaking more slowly Corrina tried again. 'You have spoken English before?'

Nabob nodded smiling broadly. 'Men on ship. They talk, I listen. I speak.'

'You were on the ship a long time?'

'Long, long time, Missie. Me learn

to speak plenty. Me listen hard.'

'Did you want to stay in England?'

The Blackamoor grinned widely. 'Nabob very happy with Missie. Nabob work hard. Try and please Missie.'

Corrina smiled. She was delighted with her Blackamoor. He would be a far better companion than the parrot Grenville had brought her back, from some foreign port and which she remembered with distaste, had indulged in squawking fits.

With a wave of her hand she dismissed the Blackamoor. 'You may go now, Nabob. Get some food from the kitchen and then you can sleep on the mattress on the floor of my dressing-room. Tomorrow, we will see about a proper livery for you.'

Nabob grinned happily, his white teeth flashing in the light from the great silver candelabra.

'You must learn your duties. You must wait upon my demands, when we are at home; accompanying me when I visit, or go shopping, and carry any parcels, or packages, I may have with me. When I go out in my carriage you will ride on the box, between the coachman and the footman. You will jump down, and stand behind the footman, when he opens my carriage door. You will then follow closely behind me wherever I may visit, unless I tell you otherwise. Do you understand?'

Nabob smiled and bowed low, kissing Corrina's hand.

She looked steadily at the beaming black face before her. 'You will not leave this house unless I do, or unless I send you on a message. You understand?'

'Nabob very happy,' grinned the Blackamoor. 'Nabob love his Missie, do everything she ask.'

'Good. You do as I tell you always. If you misbehave you will be whipped.'

Stark terror disfigured the boy's face. He sank to his knees and held on to her skirts, whimpering with fear.

'No, no,' he whined. 'Missie not

whip Nabob. Him good boy.'

Revelling in her power, Corrina stood looking down at him, her blue eyes hard and calculating. Then she motioned him to rise.

'Do as I tell you, and remember all the instructions I have given you, and you will come to no harm.'

Smiles again wreathed his black, round face.

'Go now,' she instructed.

Walking backwards, and bowing low in subservience to her wishes, Nabob left the room.

11

As soon as it was dawn and light enough for him to find the path back over the Moss, Jim Grenville returned to Wallasey.

Angered by Matt's behaviour, he had declined to stay at the Ring o' Bells. Instead, he had sheltered in a farm outhouse until it was light enough for him to find his way back across the Moss.

The early morning was cold and sunless. The harsh cry of the gulls and the cold swish of the ebbing tide were the only sounds that assailed his ears. He heard a cock crow as he passed through the village of Liscard, but there was no thin curl of smoke from any of the cottages, and no sign of human life.

He entered Mother Redcap's tavern silently. The back door was unlatched and he silently blessed Melany for her thoughtfulness.

He was startled though, when entering the kitchen, to find her there waiting for him. She was huddled on the great oak settle, wrapped in a grey blanket. She placed her fingers warningly over her lips.

'Hush! My Aunt is a light sleeper.' Cautiously she slid off the settle. Her legs were cramped from her long vigil and she would have stumbled against the table if he had not caught her in his arms. She sank her weight against him and sobbed on his chest.

'I was afraid you mightn't return. I've waited all night for you. Once I thought of following you, but I knew that I should be unable to overtake you, and even if I did you would never have listened to me.'

Jim stroked her dark head soothingly. 'There, there,' he murmured. 'I'm back safely. There is nothing to fear. The Moss is not nearly so bad as I was led to believe. I had a little trouble crossing the Jawbones but it's all right now.'

She pulled back in his arms and raising a tear-stained face looked at him incredulously.

'You mean you don't know what danger you've been in. How very near death you've been this night? Did you deliver your parcel to the Ring o' Bells?'

Grenville's face darkened as he recalled the episode.

'Yes,' he said curtly, 'I delivered the parcel but it didn't contain the contraband I was led to believe it did. There are several points I want enlightenment on.'

'Enlightenment on!' Melany repeated the words after him in a whisper before breaking into semi-hysterical sobs. She clung to Jim sobbing, and crying, and trying to stifle the sounds by burying her face on his chest.

'Thank God! You've got back safely. Thank God! they let you escape. Didn't they press you to stay at the Ring o' Bells until daylight?'

'They did but I was annoyed over the parcel so I refused to stay. I spent several hours under a hayrick. Then, as soon as it was light enough to find the Jawbones, and the path over the Moss, I made my way back here.'

Melany stared at him in amazement.

'You've had a near escape from death,' she blurted out. 'After you left here yesterday evening a horseman arrived. He spoke to my Aunt and asked for Matt. My Aunt showed him into our sitting-room and sent Matt to him. They ordered drinks and when I took them in I saw that the gentleman talking with Matt was Lord Pendleton. I recognised him as the gentleman who had been in the carriage with Corrina the day I went to Liverpool. They were talking very confidentially about something, and as I entered with the drinks they stopped. Lord Pendleton was seated with his back towards me and it was not till I was setting the tankards down that he saw me. He recognised me at once and said: 'Why, we meet again!' Matt expressed surprise that we had ever met. Lord Pendleton then told him of the circumstances of our meeting in Liverpool. Then, he turned to me and said: 'Let's see, it was something about a Captain Grenville, who was from a ship that had been wrecked called . . . ' He paused for a moment, as if trying to recall the name of the ship, and Matt prompted him with, 'the *Golden Lady*.' '

I quickly put their drinks down and excused myself, pretending not to hear him ask your whereabouts. I knew Matt was watching me closely and I felt sure he knew our secret. After that I kept busy in the other room.

In a little while Matt and Lord Pendleton moved into the room where I was serving. They caused quite a stir. More than one of Matt's men were sizing up Lord Pendleton. What with the diamond pin and the diamond rings on his fingers and the fine lace at his neck and cuffs he must have looked a prize worth taking. If he'd been with anyone but Matt he would have needed to use the pair of bejewelled pistols he wore in the belt round his waist. As soon as I could I slipped away to try and warn you but you'd already left and I was afraid to follow you in case Matt guessed where I'd gone.

It was close on midnight when Lord Pendleton left, and almost at once Matt disappeared.

Lord Pendleton left a note with my Aunt and asked her to give it to me. Here,' she held out a crumpled piece of paper, 'read it.'

> 'It is unwise to become involved with wreckers, especially to work against them. I should hate to see a pretty wench come to any harm. After tonight you will never see Captain Grenville again. For your own sake don't seek him. Destroy this note and forget any suspicions you may have. Matt will not question you.
>
> 'P'.

Jim crumpled the piece of paper and thrust it into his pocket.

'So, Matt knows,' he said softly. 'That was why Matt was there to greet me. Why then did he let me go so easily?'

'Perhaps he thought you might drown in the bog on your return journey.'

Jim shook his head thoughtfully. 'If I crossed it once then surely I could re-cross it. He must have some other motive for letting me remain free and alive.'

'But what are you going to do. Has anyone seen you enter here. Did you pass anyone on the way back?'

Jim shook his head. 'Not a soul was stirring as I came through the village.'

Fresh hope surged in Melany. 'You must hide before my Aunt wakens. There are plenty of secret places in this house. I will let her think that you have disappeared. When my Aunt or Matt question me I will say that I have not seen you since last night. You must remain in hiding until we can find out what Matt's plans are. I may be mistaken but I think that Lord Pendleton is in some way connected with the wrecking of the *Golden Lady*.'

Jim looked slightly incredulous.

'But, if that's the case, why didn't he warn Matt, before now, that I was alive. He even knew I was here.'

'I don't understand that myself. Perhaps he thought it didn't matter. There are dozens of reasons why he didn't do so. The point to remember is that he has done so now, and that you're in peril as a result.'

'And you?'

She shook her dark head. 'Not if you do as I say. You must remain in hiding. I will bring you food, and drink, when I can, and in the meantime I will find out what Matt's plans are.'

'But how? Matt isn't likely to trust you knowing that you befriended me.'

Melany smiled. 'You are forgetting Sammy.'

'You mean . . . ?'

'I mean that Sammy promised to

buy me a present — a worthy present — as soon as Matt shared out the loot from the *Golden Lady*. Well, now I intend to see that Sammy keeps that promise. It should be easy enough. He is kind-hearted and won't easily break his word. In the meantime I may even be able to encourage him to tell other information we want.'

Jim looked down into her eager dark eyes, smiling a little wryly. 'You maybe are right, Melany, but somehow I don't like it. If anything goes wrong. If Matt ever suspects you . . . '

Before he could finish there was a sound of movement from the room above.

'Quick!' Melany began to hustle him from the room. 'It's my Aunt. She is awake, and will be down here in a few minutes. You must hide.'

'But Melany . . . '

Holding her fingers up for silence she pushed him towards the fireplace and ran her hand over the rough stonework. A pillar began to swing inwards. 'In there,' she whispered. She thrust the blanket she had been wrapped in towards him.

'Take this, it will help to keep you warm. Later I will try and get you another one.'

Darting across the room she went behind the bar and filled a tankard with ale. She thrust this into his hand and went back to fetch a small bottle of rum, a hunk of bread and some cheese.

'Here,' she thrust the food towards him. 'Now get inside quickly. The tunnel leads to the Red Nose caves,' she whispered. 'If you ever need to you can escape that way. For the present stay this end of the tunnel and I'll bring you some more food and a lantern later today.'

Not waiting for his reply she swung the great stone back into position and slipped from the room before her Aunt came down the stairs.

12

Corrina expressed surprise when the carriage in which she and Lord Pendleton were driving pulled up at Liverpool's Quayside adjacent to a large, flat-bottomed ferry boat. As if complying with some pre-arranged plan the coachman proceeded to lead his horses down the wide gangplank onto the boat itself.

'What is happening?' Corrina asked, a puzzled look in her blue eyes.

'We're merely crossing to the Cheshire side,' Pendleton told her. 'I thought a breath of country air would be enjoyable.'

'But surely, there is country air to be gained this side of the water? Besides,' she continued, feigning petulance, 'I'm not a good sailor, and neither is Nabob. In fact, I think we had better let him come inside the carriage with us. The cold from the water might affect him.'

'By all means have him inside if you wish it.'

He waited until the little Blackamoor, resplendent in his scarlet and gold livery, had been summoned and had taken a stool at their feet inside the carriage.

'I have a surprise for you,' murmured Pendleton, when they were once more settled.

'Indeed! A pleasant one I hope.' Corrina flickered her lashes provocatively.

'I trust you will think it so.'

She looked at him questioningly. He was lying back against the rich maroon upholstery of the carriage. His eyes were half shut and he was regarding her closely. His mouth was twisted in an expression that could have been a smile, or a sneer. For a moment she felt afraid of him, and wondered how she could possibly be entertaining the thought of marriage to such a man. His chin was weak and receding, his nose sharp and long, and the skin of his face so pale as to give the appearance of fragility, or ill-health. For a moment she wondered if he would still possess the same attraction if he was deprived of his title. Yet there was something about him that commanded her attention. It was partly the veiled cruelty that showed in his face, in the sneering smile that played round his thin mouth, and the calculating coldness of his eyes, that excited her.

'Are you going to tell me more about it?'

'If I did it would hardly be a surprise.'

He glanced through the carriage windows. The Wallasey coast loomed near. The village of Seacombe, huddling over the landing stage like a broody hen, looked uninviting. Further along the coast the sun shone on the golden expanse of sand, which disappeared into the wide open moor, hiding Liscard from view. It looked barren countryside; but with the sun shining, the sand glinting, and a few gulls and plovers wheeling overhead there was a freshness about the scene that was exhilarating.

Their arrival at Seacombe caused quite a stir. Eventually, after much cursing, and swearing, the feat of getting their coach and horses from boat to land was accomplished. In no time they were trotting along the rough road between Seacombe and Liscard.

'And now pray, what is the surprise?' Corrina asked again, her curiosity whetted.

'All in good time, all in good time.'

She tried to conceal her impatience. 'Shall we lower a window?' she asked. 'If it was intended that I should enjoy the country air then we had better permit a little of it to enter the carriage.'

Bowing gallantly he complied with her wishes.

'Pray, do not let it ruffle your charming appearance,' he begged. 'After I have shown you the countryside I have arranged that we should lunch with my cousin the Vicar of St. Hilary's church. I think you will enjoy his company.'

'Indeed!' She looked askance. 'I did not know you were acquainted with the gentleman. I have heard rumours that he is . . . ' she hesitated, as if searching for the right words to express herself.

Pendleton waited patiently, as if he did not know what it was she was trying to say.

'I have heard,' she blurted out at length, 'That for a clergyman he keeps singularly queer company. That he is not above mixing with the smugglers and the like.'

Pendleton pursed his lips thoughtfully before replying.

'Doubtless a Vicar will have many unsavoury types amongst his flock in a place like this,' he said evasively. 'If he is a good Vicar then surely he must tolerate them, the sinners along with the saved.'

'Quite, quite. I am not reproaching the good Vicar for doing what must be his duty; but it is rumoured that he goes even further. On occasion he has been known, if not to help them, then at least to aid them in their escape. Even to help to conceal their loot upon occasions.'

'Really!' Pendleton smoothed the chamois gloves over his long thin hands, thoughtfully. 'You know of this for a fact?'

'Well, no. Not for a fact. I have heard men talk when they have been dining with my father and many are the wild and dreadful things they say takes place on this side of the water.'

Pendleton laughed, and leaning forward patted her hand consolingly. 'Don't worry your pretty head about such things. Men speculate a great deal when they have only rumour to go upon. Probably the Vicar of St. Hilary's would be just as surprised as you are at the tales concerning his conduct. You might tell him some of them and perhaps he will be able to confirm them, or disprove them.'

'Oh no, I shouldn't dream of doing

such a thing.' Corrina looked aghast at the suggestion. 'If he is a relative of yours then I am quite sure it will be right and proper for us to lunch with him; and that his character is above reproach.'

Pendleton smiled but did not deign to reply. Corrina turned her attention to the view from the carriage window. They were approaching a village and women, with children in arms, or clutching at their skirts, came to stand at their cottage doors to watch the fine carriage and pair drive past.

'Causing quite a stir,' remarked Pendleton with a smirk.

Corrina smiled assent. 'Seems strange that 'tis so quiet and peaceful. These cottages with their well tended gardens, the hedgerows aglow with wild flowers, the birds singing, and the sun shining, it all seems so peaceful. It is hard to think that only a mile or so away the sea is thundering up the beaches and that such dreadful things as smuggling and wrecking are carried on.'

Pendleton's face hardened: 'Why trouble your pretty head about such happenings then if you think them unpleasant.'

Corrina sighed: ' 'Twas but a passing thought.'

'And no doubt it was accompanied by a passing thought of Captain Grenville.'

Corrina started at the chill that had pierced his voice.

'Why no! I must confess I hadn't thought of him at all.'

'Not at all?' persisted Pendleton. 'Not since the day the wench from the tavern, over here, brought you news of him?'

He noted her hesitancy. 'Come, come, my pretty Corrina. I am too old a friend of yours to be deceived. I know you have been thinking of this handsome, red-headed Captain. In fact, there has been a marked change in you since the day the news was brought that he was alive and well.'

'Really, Sir,' Corrina drew herself up

in annoyance. 'I can see no reason why I should be answerable to you on such a matter. All the same, I can assure you . . . '

'That it would be nice to see him once again,' finished Pendleton.

'What do you mean?'

'Just this, my dear. You may have wondered when I am going to broach the matter of our marriage, with your father. Well, the truth is I should have done it earlier. Since hearing that Captain Grenville is still alive I have made one or two enquiries. I find that I was not mistaken. At one time there was a great affection between you both.

When I learned that he was still alive I was anxious to clear all doubt both from your mind, and my own, that you no longer held him in the same esteem. I wanted to assure myself that it was I, and I alone, that you now held dear to you.'

'Well, really . . . '

Pendleton signalled her to keep silent.

'Hence this little outing to pay your Captain a visit. He will no doubt be overjoyed to see you again, and you . . . Well, we will discuss your reactions after we have met the Captain.

If you look through the window you can see the sea again. We have but half a mile downhill to go and we shall be at Mother Redcap's tavern. If the wench who spoke to us in Liverpool told the truth 'tis there that we should see your Captain.'

'But that was many weeks ago. He may have left there.'

'What! Without ever having contacted you.' Her cheeks flushed as he raised his eyebrows in disbelief.

13

Melany could barely wait for Jim to answer her signal before she began to pour out the story of Corrina, and Lord Pendleton's visit.

Whilst he sat on the settle, before the dying embers of the fire, ravenously eating the food she had acquired for him, she told him in detail of their visit.

Melany described how her Aunt had whisked a clean white apron round her middle and hurried forward to greet Lord Pendleton and Corrina as they had stepped from their fine carriage with a Blackamoor in attendance. She mimicked Lord Pendleton's imperious tones as he had called: 'Mother Redcap, you have staying here a sailor, a Sea Captain by the name of Grenville — Jim Grenville. Acquaint him of our presence and tell him to present himself to us at once.'

'When she went up to your room and found that you weren't there she was in a terrible panic. She called down to me. I was out in the back feeding the chickens. I hadn't reckoned on her asking after you so soon and I hadn't a story ready. I said that you must have gone for a walk. I said I would see if you were walking on the strand in front of the house, and ran off to look before she could question me further.

I thought it must be Matt, or one of his men, who were asking after you and of course after making a pretence of looking along the beach I went back into the tavern, by the front door. You can imagine my horror when I saw who was there.

They both recognised me and Pendleton said, 'Well, here's the wench who first brought us news of your Captain, my dear Corrina. If any one should know of his whereabouts she should.'

Before I could reply who should walk in but Matt. He looked startled when he saw the company. Pendleton turned and saw him immediately and I thought he was going to speak to him. On both their faces was a look of recognition yet neither of them spoke to the other.

Matt took a seat as nearby as he dared, but Pendleton looked away from him and went on questioning me about your whereabouts. The awful part of it all was that both my Aunt and Matt were within earshot and Lord Pendleton was making it so clear that I had been in touch with him, and Corrina, about you. I don't know what I said but Pendleton jested that I was attempting to conceal your whereabouts in order to annoy Corrina. She didn't speak at all, just looked as if she disbelieved every word I said.

It was terrible, Jim. I was so scared lest I should say something to give you away, either to Matt, or to them. I had to say that I hadn't seen you since the previous evening. My Aunt told me that your bed hadn't been slept in. She seemed surprised to hear you were the Captain of the *Golden Lady*.

All the time Matt was listening to what was being said and I felt his eyes on me when Pendleton told them that I had crossed to Liverpool to tell Corrina that you were still alive.

Of course my Aunt wanted to know how I knew you were the Captain of the *Golden Lady*.

It was terrible, Jim, with Matt sitting there listening. I had to admit that I had known all along who you really were and that I had gone to Liverpool with the intention of letting Cornelius Tobin and Corrina know of your whereabouts.

When Corrina said they were going to visit Lord Pendleton's cousin, the Vicar of St. Hilary's church, Matt disappeared. Later I saw him getting into their carriage. Before they left Pendleton said that if you came back before three o'clock I was to take you along to the Vicarage. If you didn't return before that time I was to come along and they would give me a message for you. My Aunt, of course, agreed readily enough.'

Melany broke off in her story to admonish Jim to eat and drink the food she had brought him.

'Do hurry in case my Aunt should hear a noise and come down to see what is happening. If she comes you must slip back through the wall as quickly as you can. I'll close the panel. Leave the dishes here, if she were to miss any, now that her suspicions of you are aroused, she would guess I had hidden you somewhere. She knows all the secret hiding places in this house and she wouldn't rest until she had unearthed you. She would do it to help Matt. She thinks him a fine fellow and would stop at nothing to help him, as you well know.'

'Go on talking. I am ravenously hungry, and thirsty, but your tale keeps me from my food.'

'Well, in that case, I shall remain silent until you've eaten.'

‘For God’s sake go on,’ said Jim impatiently. ‘I’m all on edge. Go on with your story. I’ll eat, as well as listen to you, and listen for your Aunt as well.’

Melany sighed. ‘Well, there’s not really very much more to tell.’

‘But didn’t they give you a message to give to me?’ asked Jim anxiously. ‘Didn’t . . . didn’t Corrina give you a message for me?’

Melany shook her head. ‘No, she didn’t.’ Then, noticing his crestfallen face, she went on hurriedly. ‘How could she. It was so obvious that the others didn’t want you for any friendly reason. I think she was as surprised as I was to find out their true nature.’

‘Their true nature. What do you mean?’

‘Well, you can judge that from their message to you.’

‘You haven’t told me yet what their message was.’

‘Oh dear.’ Melany became flushed and confused. ‘Interrupting me, like you've done, has upset the thread of my story. How far had I got?'

'You had just reached the point where you were in the drawing-room at the vicarage and Lord Pendleton was going to give you a message for me.'

'Oh yes. Well, he asked me whether I thought it unusual that you had been absent for so long. I just said I didn't know.

Then Matt spoke to him in a very quiet voice. I couldn't hear what was said, but I have no doubt that he was explaining what had happened last night, and about the mission you had gone on for them. The Vicar and Pendleton seemed very amused.'

'And what about Corrina?'

'She chose that moment to admonish her Blackamoor about something and did not appear to take any interest in what was going on.'

'And then.'

'They all seemed to be laughing. Lord Pendleton said to me 'When next you see your friend, Captain Grenville, tell him that we are most interested in his health, and welfare, and we hope to see him very soon. Tell him we can hardly wait for the pleasure of his company'.

They all laughed when he said this, that is all except Corrina. She seemed to have lost interest in the whole affair and was yawning.

Lord Pendleton then stood up and said he must be leaving and said we could ride with them some of the way. When Matt and me left the coach at Liscard, Lord Pendleton reminded me to deliver the message to you as soon as possible. He said, next time he called he would expect you to be there.

Matt seemed very amused by this and he and Lord Pendleton parted on the best of terms, and in high spirits.'

Jim was silent after she had finished.

Melany collected the empty dishes, and took them into the kitchen. Returning to where he was crouched over the fire, she said softly, 'Jim, I'm sorry but I don't think it is safe for you to stay here talking any longer.'

'No. You're quite right,' he replied. 'You get back to bed now. Is there any way we could meet tomorrow, before night time I mean. I must plan something. I wish I knew what Matt was up to. You've not found anything out from Sammy?'

Melany shook her head. 'No, I've not seen Sammy since I promised to get information from him. I don't want to hurry things or my aunt, and Matt, might get suspicious. You see . . . ' she paused awkwardly searching for the right words, 'you see, I've never shown interest in anyone before and I don't quite know how to go about it.'

With a groan Jim gathered her into his arms.

'Melany, my darling,' his lips moved tenderly over her face and neck. 'I know how much you are doing for me. I shall never, never forget your devotion. Pray God, I may be worthy of it. Help me, my darling, you are the only friend I have in the world.

While I have been shut up in this tunnel all day only the thought that you were working, and helping me, has kept me sane. I've wanted to storm into the tavern and confront Matt, and his gang of black devils. Now, from what you've told me, it looks as though Matt is just a pawn in a scheme of even greater evil than I had imagined existed. Between us, my darling, we've got to break this chain, punish these criminals and justify our doubts. You shall not go unrewarded my sweet angel.'

Raising her lips to his, Melany whispered. 'You must go now, my darling. It is unsafe to stay here longer. All the reward I want is that I shall succeed in helping you.'

For several minutes they clung together. Melany almost swooning with love. Her heart pounded as he kissed her eyes, her cheeks, her hair where it was swept back at the temples, and where it nestled into the nape of her neck.

Then, at last, after a long and lingering kiss on her lips, he released her and stepped back into the darkness of the tunnel.

'Goodbye, my darling,' she whispered, 'I will try and be at the Red Noses entrance to the tunnel, at about three tomorrow afternoon. It's easy for you to find. Follow the passage you're in for about half a mile, then follow it to the left. Keep well out of sight at the Red Noses. I will let you know I'm there by singing 'Greensleeves' as I approach.'

14

Back in Liverpool Corrina retired early to her room. She complained to her father that the journey to and from Wallasey had tired her and had brought on a headache. He was most solicitous. She was the pivot his life revolved around. A widower, he managed his affairs with the sole purpose of providing Corrina with the very best that money could provide. He thought her the most beautiful woman he had ever known — even more beautiful than her mother had been when he had first married her.

To his mind Corrina had inherited the best qualities from both of them. She had her mother's brilliant eyes, that could sparkle provocatively, or become sea-blue depths of mystery; she had her mother's soft golden hair and delicate colouring; but it was from him she had gained stature that showed her shapely figure to such a fine advantage. The gowns she wore — always of costly satin or silk — clung to her supple curves as if they had been moulded on her. Cornelius often dallied with the idea of employing a craftsman to carve a figure-head in her likeness to place on his ships. There was something just a little improper about the idea and this restrained him.

He knew that with the fortune that would be her wedding dowry he could afford to pick and choose a husband for her. He watched the affair between Corrina and Lord Pendleton with mixed feelings. True it would be a great honour for his daughter to marry into nobility, yet Lord Pendleton was not the kind of man that he wanted to fill that role. Cornelius Tobin considered himself to be a judge of men and there was something cruel and calculating in the man's manner that he disliked. Another thing that irked him was Pendleton's dandified appearance and manners. Brought up in a hard school himself, he liked men of stamina and spirit. He himself, by the age of twenty-two, had owned his own boat. In the space of seven years he had built up a fleet that sailed under his flag in every ocean of the world.

As he sat alone in his oak panelled study, a massive, impressive figure, in a red velvet smoking jacket, his feet resting on the richly carved mantelpiece, he brooded on the matter. A blaze of logs filled the room with warmth, and dispelled the chill of the early evening. As he drew thoughtfully on his pipe he thought again of Jim Grenville. He had liked Grenville and he was more than sorry that he should have come to such a grievous end, within such a short distance of home. It was the loss of Grenville more than the loss of the *Golden Lady*, and the treasure she was carrying, that had perturbed him when he had first heard the news.

If Grenville had returned with the

treasure, even if it had not proved to be as great as he expected, there was no reason at all why Corrina and Grenville shouldn't have been married. The girl seemed genuinely fond of Grenville, and he of her. Grenville himself was a man after Tobin's own heart. God-fearing — yet fearing no man. Resolute and determined in the face of danger. Resourceful, and a leader of men.

'By God!' Cornelius smote his thigh, and spoke aloud to the glowing heart of the fire. 'I bet he showed those wreckers. I warrant he put up a rare fight when it came to the end. Would that I had been there to see it.'

Still muttering aloud he rose from his deep leather chair and began pacing the room.

'He would have been a better man than that lily-livered Pendleton. I'll swear it's only her money he's after. I've heard rumours as how he's so poor that it's only his title that keeps him in favour with his creditors, and many's the shady deal, and gambling scandal he's been mixed up in. It's his title that has turned Corrina's head.'

He sighed sadly. If only Grenville had returned. With the money and the backing I could have given them, they would have held a place of respect in Liverpool equal to any title, he thought.

Alone in her own sumptuous room Corrina's thoughts were running along very similar lines to those of her father.

She had dismissed her blackamoor and had partly undressed. Wearing a loose gown of pale blue silk, edged with swansdown, she reclined on the enormous sheepskin rug before the log fire, munching at an apple and dipping into a dish of sweatmeats by her side. Thinking over the events of the day, she wondered whether to take her father into her confidence. It would mean telling him that not only was Grenville still alive, but that he had actually tried to contact them some two months ago, just shortly after the *Golden Lady* had been wrecked.

Knowing her father's regard for Grenville, and distress at losing Grenville, she would have to be very clever to explain away her long delay in not mentioning the matter earlier.

Of course, she had no positive proof that Grenville was alive except that the old woman who kept the tavern on the Cheshire side had seemed surprised that he was out. The girl Melany, who had sought her out in Liverpool, and had claimed to have nursed Grenville back to health had also been there. She had seemed to think he was probably only out walking on the shore.

Then there had been the visit to Pendleton's cousin, the Vicar of St. Hilary's. A shiver ran through her as she recalled their meeting. She had sensed something sinister about him and felt that he was laughing at her the entire time she was in his company.

When Pendleton had explained the reason for their visit, there had been an exchange of glances that she had been unable to fathom. They had taken

Melany to the vicarage with them and also a fierce-looking bearded man of massive build and coarse ways. When they had met him earlier, at Mother Redcap's, he had neither spoken to Pendleton nor Pendleton to him. Yet, at the vicarage both Pendleton and his cousin seemed to be on familiar terms with him.

For a long time Corrina lay curled on the sheepskin rug until the fire began to die low in the hearth, and a chilliness crept into the room making her shiver, and draw her wrap more closely round her shoulders.

Exasperated because she had solved none of the problems chasing round in her head, she prepared for bed. As she drifted off to sleep her thoughts were of Grenville, not Lord Pendleton. The Jim Grenville she had known some two summers ago, before he had set sail on his fateful voyage in the *Golden Lady*. She saw again his tall broad figure, his fiery shock of auburn hair. She dreamed his arms were holding her close and that once again he was kissing her as he had done on the night before his departure.

Tears began to seep beneath her tightly-shut lids. Tears of pity that she was separated from such a lover and only consoled by the insipid love-making and soft embraces of Lord Pendleton.

The thought that perhaps the wench at Mother Redcap's was Grenville's paramour filled her with a mad fever. She must go over to Wallasey again. She must see the girl alone. If Grenville was alive she must see him. The desire to be crushed once again to his strong chest burned within her, until she thought she would swoon from desire. Just to see him, to feel him touch her and once more to look into his eyes and see the love he had for her burning there, blotted all reason from her mind.

She refused to let herself think that perhaps he no longer loved her. Doubtless the girl had helped him because she was infatuated by his looks. She is probably in love with him, she thought smugly, but Jim would not forget me so easily. I will seek him out, or failing that, seek out the girl and get her to give him a message.

Instinctively Corrina knew that she must do it without Pendleton knowing. His interest boded no good for Jim, of that she felt certain.

Still blissfully contemplating her reunion with Grenville, Corrina settled more comfortably between the soft sheets and drifted off to sleep.

15

A week passed before Melany had any definite news for Jim Grenville. A week that was filled with frustration and anxiety. Jim, who was still hiding in the secret tunnel that led from Mother Redcap's tavern to the caves, fretted and worried at his inactivity.

On the other side of the thick stone wall Melany spent the long days helping her aunt to clean the tavern, feed their few livestock, and dispense the home brewed ale, for which the tavern was famed. She did not find it easy to act carefree. She was too conscious of Matt's speculative gaze and wondered how much he knew or suspected. She was nervous too lest her aunt should notice that food disappeared, or might hear the creaking of the stairs, as she crept down for her nightly rendezvous with Jim.

After the first few attempts the plan to meet by day, near the Red Noses, had been abandoned. There were too many people about looking for flotsam or jetsam, which the receding tide left high on the shore. Once she had encountered Matt and it had frightened her a great deal, making her even more wary and cautious.

On this night, however, as she swung back the heavy stone slab that concealed the entrance, and gave the pre-arranged signal for Jim to come out from his hiding place, and eat the food and drink she had brought for him, she felt elated. Her eyes were shining and there was a smile of welcome on her face. Jim at once sensed her apparent eagerness to impart news.

'Let's hear it,' he grinned. 'I was all ready to have a good grumble, but the sight of your face, looking like a flood of sunshine after an April shower, has driven my ill humour clean away.'

He gathered her into his arms and pressed his lips to hers.

Gently, but impatiently, she pushed him away. Much as she enjoyed the ardour of his love-making she felt it was not the right moment for it. She was sure, too, that Jim would share her feelings once she had told him her news.

She handed him the food she was carrying.

'Begin eating this,' she ordered, 'and listen carefully. Every minute is urgent. I tried to come down earlier but my aunt was late retiring and I had to be sure she was asleep before I risked it.'

Grenville took the meat patty she held out to him, and the tankard of ale. He had not tasted food since the previous night and he was ravenous, and did full justice to her offerings.

She watched with pleasure, then leaning towards him, and speaking in a low, but urgent voice said,

'Now, listen carefully. I have reason to believe that tonight Matt and his men will move the treasure they took from the *Golden Lady*!'

Jim stopped eating to stare incredulously at her.

'How have you found out?' he gasped.

Food was forgotten, his eyes were agleam at the thought of squaring his debt with the wreckers.

Noticing this Melany stopped her flood of words. 'You must eat,' she admonished, 'or you will not have the strength to act against these men. Remember, you have been shut up in this tunnel for a week now, without light or fresh air, and with only a minimum of food; whereas Matt's men not only outnumber you but they are strong and cunning. You will need all the energy you can summon up to outwit them. Little use my imparting the knowledge I have if you faint when the time comes for action.'

Annoyance and indignation darkened Grenville's face.

'Faint!' He exploded the word angrily. 'Am I a woman to faint when courage is called for? When I encounter these dastardly wreckers I'll smash the skulls of every man of them.'

It was Melany's turn to look contemptuous. 'Fine talk,' she said angrily. 'Single handed you talk of smashing in the heads of some fifteen or twenty men. All of whom will be armed with clubs, and knives, and who are strong and fit into the bargain. Less than a month ago you were hovering on the brink of death. If you think that you can recover your treasure, and overcome the wreckers, by sheer force then I shall not waste further time telling you the details of their plans.'

'For God's sake, Melany, if you love me, or for that matter if you have any feelings at all for me, tell me all you know and let me settle the matter in my own way.'

'It's because I love you, Jim, that I refuse to let you sacrifice your life.'

In the glow of the dying fire her dark eyes looked enormous and he saw that they were wet with unshed tears.

Gently he took her hands in his.

'My darling, my little Melany,' he said softly, drawing her close to him. 'I won't do anything that is reckless or headstrong. I know what your feelings for me are, and I feel as deeply towards you. It is just that I am so anxious to settle my debt with these scoundrels that I appear to be foolhardy. Tell me what you know, and I will endeavour to outwit them by cunning as crafty as that of their own devising. I promise you I will not take one single chance that may seem foolish. Nor will I run the risk of being caught, or of involving you in the matter.'

Blinking away her tears she told him, 'I learned the news from Sammy. You remember he promised to buy me a handsome present as soon as they shared out the loot taken from the *Golden Lady*.

'I saw him last night and I reminded him of his promise. He seemed surprised — probably because I was so off hand with him when he first made the offer. As you know, in the past I haven't encouraged his attentions. It's not that he isn't a very nice boy, it's just that . . . '

Jim pressed her hand to signify that he understood what she was trying to say, and Melaney continued.

'He said it might be sooner than I expected. He'd had rather more to drink than was good for him, and the ale loosened his tongue. He looked round the room and seeing Matt wasn't there he told me that he and about fifteen of Matt's men had been told to assemble this very night at the Yellow Noses. He knew, from what he had overheard Matt saying to some of the others, that they were going to collect the loot from HIM.'

'HIM? Who did he mean?'

'I don't know. I always thought that Matt was the head of the gang but it seems that there is someone in higher authority than Matt. Someone who gives orders to Matt.'

Jim was silent for a minute. When he spoke it was almost to himself. 'Yes,' he said, 'I understand about that. Matt is the leader of the men but there is a higher brain behind the organisation. Someone who disposes of the goods they capture, after the excitement had died down. It is probably someone who also has some knowledge of the ships which are expected into the port. It might be someone on this side or it might even be someone in Liverpool, even connected with the Customs in an official capacity.' He noticed that she was shaking her head. 'You have some other idea? What is it then?'

She hesitated for a moment, as if reluctant to speak. Her dark eyes searched his face in a constrained manner. Then, she said hesitantly, 'You know, Jim, ever since that afternoon when Corrina Tobin and Lord Pendleton called here asking for you I have been trying to understand what was going on between Lord Pendleton and Matt. How was it that he didn't seem to know Matt when they were here and yet at St. Hilary's vicarage Lord Pendleton spoke with Matt as if he had known him for a long long time.

I think he and Matt do know each other. I think that somewhere there is a connection between Matt, and Lord Pendleton, and the vicar of St. Hilary's and the wreckers.'

Jim looked at her in astonishment. 'You mean you think that Lord Pendleton is the one who is giving Matt his orders?'

'Either that, or even more likely, it is his cousin, the Vicar, who is issuing the orders. And he could be receiving information from Lord Pendleton about the ships due to arrive in port. Because of his standing, he would be in a position to obtain such information and because of the Vicar's position over here he, too, is above suspicion.'

Jim looked thoughtful and for several minutes ate in silence. Setting down his empty tankard, he exclaimed, 'It sounds preposterous, Melany, but you know there is just a chance that you may be right. And do you think that they are hiding the loot and contraband in the church somewhere?'

'Either in the church or in the vaults underneath. After all, no one is likely to pry around there. Most people are too afraid of encountering ghosts, especially after dark, to even go near the graveyard. Another thing, the church stands so high that it would make a fine look-out point. You can see far along the coast and into the channel from the high ground it stands on, and if one climbed up into the tower itself the view would be even better.'

Grenville looked at her in admiration. 'The smugglers should have you on their side, you would be a great asset to them.'

She smiled at his praise, and her cheeks became flushed.

'I may be quite wrong, I have no proof, of course.'

He nodded thoughtfully.

'There is only one point which worries me. If Lord Pendleton is in league with the smugglers, and was coming over to make plans with his cousin regarding the treasure taken from the *Golden Lady*, why did he bring Corrina with him.'

'But don't you see that was done on purpose.' Melany leant towards him, her eyes sparking earnestly.

'He knew you were still alive, because of my visit to Liverpool. It is probably because of that that there has been such a long delay in sharing out, and disposing of, the treasure. If you were still alive you could be dangerous. They had to make sure first of all that it was you in hiding here. So, Pendleton brought Corrina along, probably thinking that if he was present when you met he would know from her reaction whether you were Captain Jim Grenville, and not just some other member of the crew of the *Golden Lady* who was pretending to be you.

In the meantime, Matt had taken matters into his own hands. Pretending to have believed the story my aunt told him about you he agreed to test you out so that you could join his gang. That was when he arranged for you to carry some contraband to the Ring o' Bells. Neither his plans, nor those of Lord Pendleton, worked out. I imagine the conclusion they have both reached is that you perished somewhere in the Moss. This is why they think it is safe to carry on with their own plans for the disposal of the treasure.'

Grenville looked at her in astonishment. 'You have certainly chartered it all very neatly,' he said.

'I've spent a great deal of time thinking about it and wondering which is the best way for you to attempt to outwit them.'

He waited, but she made no attempt to elaborate. She sat staring into the dying embers of the fire, her hair falling loosely, so that most of her face was in shadow.

16

A fresh breeze swept in over the rugged Wirral coast from the Irish Sea, and the gentle swish of the turning tide sounded like a song on the still night air. There was a sense of anticipation in the air, felt to the full by the five men waiting in the shadows of the yellow sandstone rocks. The tide was already turning, leaving the dry sand at their feet untouched and powdery. They were straining their ears intently, listening for the signal that would tell them that the night was favourable for the deed they were to undertake. It would assure them that the honest inhabitants of Seacombe, Liscard and Wallasey were abed and sleeping soundly. It would also tell them that the Preventive officers, from Liverpool, were not prowling the shore, watching to see if any contraband was being smuggled inland.

All five of them were listening intently for the signal. Dark, swarthy men, dressed like fishermen, silent and morose in manner, cautious and hesitant in speech.

The long vigil was telling on their nerves. First one, and then another, would wet his lips, open his mouth, or clear his throat, as if he was about to speak. A slight sound from off-shore, or a glance from one of his neighbours, would make him relapse into an uneasy silence.

Suddenly, from out of the stillness, a figure materialised, startling the waiting men who as one pressed themselves back into the sheltering shadows of the cave. Then the figure moved towards the group and said in low tones, 'Everything's safe. Are you ready!'

It was a command rather than an enquiry.

'We're ready, Matt,' answered the five men who had been waiting. Matt signalled them to follow him, and leading the way inside the cave began to walk swiftly through the darkness. The others followed in single file, not speaking but each man conscious of the presence of the others. Scrabbling over the rough stone floor, keeping their heads well bent, they hurried through the darkness. The walls of the cave were rough and jagged lumps of sandstone rock poked at their clothes and faces, like so many clutching fingers.

Suddenly Matt stopped and lit a lantern. Holding it high he gazed round at his companions, who had come to a halt in a group behind him.

The part of the cave they were now in was lofty and wide, and seemed to divide up into several different passages.

'Now, here are your orders,' Matt spoke harshly, and authoritatively. 'Listen carefully. One false move and all our past work is undone. The treasure from the *Golden Lady* is the greatest we have ever captured. That is why we've all had to wait so long for our reward.'

'Why, Matt? Whatever was in that old chest that we couldn't have just shared it amongst us as we have done other times when we've had a wreck?'

Matt stared at the speaker for several minutes in complete silence. His manner made the questioner uneasy. 'Perhaps 'twould have been better if I'd not asked. Perhaps 'twere a body,' the man said with an attempted laugh, that echoed forlornly, in the cave.

'No, you have a right to ask, Pete. I know that over the past weeks all you men must have been wondering the same thing. The fact is that when that chest was opened it was found to contain a king's ransom of precious jewels.

To merely share it out would be giving each man just so many fancy baubles. Where would you, or I, for that matter, be able to sell the stuff without arousing suspicion? For many weeks now I have been trying to dispose of the treasure in return for honest gold. At last 'tis done. Tonight it is to be taken to London where we shall get a handsome exchange. After your work tonight is completed each of you will receive a token of its worth. It may be many months before the rest can be paid over. One false move and not a penny piece will there be for any of us so let no word of this pass your lips.'

The men murmured and nodded in agreement.

'Well?' Matt looked round the group. 'Are we all clear on that point, or is there anything any of you wish to say?'

No one spoke.

'Right then. Now, here are your orders for tonight. You five men have been chosen to guard the entrances to these caves. You, Pete, take the right fork to the Red Noses entrance. Conceal yourself there until you receive a message to leave — probably in about two hours' time. You, Jake, return the way we have come, and wait at the Yellow Noses. Mick, you go to the ditch behind Mother Redcap's, and keep watch there. You, Sammy, guard the tunnel that leads to Mother Redcap's tavern. I have warned her that she is not on any account to use that passage tonight. Tom, you will remain here, and allow no one to approach or pass.

Are you all clear as to what you have to do?'

The men murmured that they understood.

'Right.' Matt spoke sharply. 'To your posts then. If you meet anyone in the tunnel you are guarding, and you are unable to handle him, call out. You will be heard by Tom, who will come to your assistance. Otherwise make no move until I come back in about two hours to tell you that the job is done.

The chest with the treasure in it, has been hidden in the vaults of St. Hilary's church. The men collecting it should have started on their way here. I am going to meet them. I will give a signal to warn you of our approach, Tom. We will then carry the chest through to the Yellow Noses entrance, where I will signal Jake, to be expecting us. The rest of you should neither see or hear anything. Should you suspect anything, or you are in trouble, just shout for Tom.

Right now, to your posts. We have wasted precious time already.'

Matt waited until they had scattered, each making for the place he had been told to guard. As the sounds of their footsteps died away he handed the lantern to Tom, then vanished into the darkness, taking a way that none of the others had followed.

Tom stood alert, and listening, for several minutes. Then, judging that all was well made himself comfortable for his vigil. With his knees hunched, and his back against one of the sandstone walls, he sat waiting in case there was a shout from one of the men guarding the tunnels, or the sound of Matt's returning footsteps. The lantern made a yellow pool on the floor at his feet, it flickered slightly, as the draught in the caves made the candle gutter and spurt. All was quiet except for one dull thud that might have been someone knocking against the rough side of one of the tunnels. He waited but a hollow silence followed so he didn't investigate further.

Had he done so he would have discovered that Sammy was not at his post. Long before he reached there, as he stumbled along in the darkness a hand shot out from the gloom and seized him round his throat.

Before he could cry out for Tom to come and help him another hand had clamped down over his mouth; his legs were kicked from under him. As the jagged stone of the cave walls crashed into his skull, he heard a voice that seemed familiar. For a moment he couldn't place it, but it was a voice he had heard before under similar terrifying conditions.

This time it said, 'And let that be a lesson to you, you young pup. I didn't bargain for it to be you I should meet here tonight, you beardless babe.'

As the darkness swallowed Sammy in its enveloping arms, he knew it was the voice that had haunted him, sleeping and waking, ever since the night he had taken part in wrecking the *Golden Lady*.

He sagged limply, and lay unconscious on the floor, a few yards from the secret entrance to Mother Redcap's tavern; the entrance he was to have guarded.

A thin stream of blood, from a gash on the back of his head, where he had hit it against the jagged wall, trickled down his face as he lay unconscious on the ground.

17

Leaving Sammy's body lying on the floor of the cave, Jim Grenville crept along the tunnel. The journey seemed endless, and several times he wondered whether Sammy's presence had merely been a false alarm, or whether he would encounter the rest of the band within the next few minutes.

A faint glimmer of yellow light, as though from a lantern that had been incompletely covered, put him on his guard.

The tunnel had suddenly widened, and from where he crouched in the shadows, he could dimly see the other openings. He could also make out the outline of a figure squatting on the floor, his back against one of the walls, and his head sunk upon his chest as though deep in thought or asleep.

Moving with the agility of a cat, Jim

sprang upon the unsuspecting figure. As the man sensed his approach, and opened his mouth to shout out, Jim's hand clamped down upon it. Then raising the club he had taken from Sammy, he brought it down across the fellow's neck. The man slumped down without a sound. Rummaging through his pockets Jim found a length of stout rope, and securely tied the fellow's feet and wrists. Unceremoniously he dragged the body back into the tunnel he had just left; the tunnel where Sammy's body already lay.

Beads of perspiration poured down Grenville's face, and he mopped them away with his coat sleeve. He was sure now that Melany's news had been no false rumour, and that this was the night Matt and his gang intended to share out the treasure they had taken from the *Golden Lady*. It worried him that he may already have lost a great deal of time, and that the rest of the gang might at any moment enter the cave where he was. If only he knew where the various caves, that opened off from where he stood, led to he might have some idea which way Matt's men would come. He tried to take his bearings from the fact that the tunnel he had just come through had led from Mother Redcap's.

The two passages to the north would lead to the sea he decided while of the other two entrances one must lead inland possibly to the church itself.

He listened, but not a murmur disturbed the eerie silence of the caves. He could not even hear the sea. Quickly he decided what action to take. As he found the passage from the tavern guarded then it was more than likely that the entrances from the shore would also be guarded. It was quite possible that instead of just sharing out the treasure Matt intended to smuggle it across to Liverpool. In this case, Jim decided, the first thing to deal with were the men guarding these entrances. If he could put them out of action he would then only have to deal with the men who were bringing the chest.

His mind made up he began to move cautiously, down one of the passages which must lead to the sea.

He had travelled only a few hundred yards when he felt sand beneath his feet. Another hundred yards or so and he could hear the distant slap of the ebb tide as it licked the shingle.

A feeling of exultation filled him, yet he remained cautious. One false step, one sound to disturb the man watching at the cave entrance, and an alarm might be sounded which would be his undoing.

As soon as he saw the man on guard his hand tightened over the club he was carrying. The fellow was standing with his back to him, staring out over the shore. He seemed to be listening intently, as if for a signal that was due at any moment.

He fell silently as Jim's club descended upon his head, an inert, senseless figure on the dry sand.

Dragging the body clear of the tunnel entrance Jim paused only long enough to tie the man's hands with his own neckerchief before returning to the spot where the cave divided. Echoing from someway off he could hear the muffled tramp of men's feet. It was too late to find out if the other exits were guarded or not. For a moment he was unsure of his next move. Then, with a grim smile, he moved back into the darkness of the passage that led to Mother Redcap's and waited.

Within seconds Matt and four men appeared. Jim saw that two of them carried the heavy iron bound chest, that had been stolen from his cabin on the night of the wreck. At the sight of it his blood rose. It was all he could do to contain himself and not rush towards them, regardless of the consequences. Clenching his fists, and muttering vengeance, he forced himself to remain hidden.

Matt was leading the party and Jim heard him utter an exclamation of surprise at the sight of the lantern flickering on the ground but no sign of anyone on guard.

He heard Matt call, 'Tom, Tom, where are you?'

The caves re-echoed his cry, but there came no answer.

The two men carrying the chest shifted it uneasily.

At a glance from Matt their shuffling stopped; they remained silent, but apprehensive, looking from one to the other.

Matt called again, but his voice echoed in the silence.

'Put that box down,' instructed Matt, 'and you, Mark, stay here and guard it. The rest of us will check up with the men posted at the entrances.

'I'll go through to Jake at the Yellow Noses. You, Harry, check on Pete, at the Red Noses. Charlie, see if Mick is still at the ditch behind Mother Redcap's. That leaves only the entrance that leads to the tavern itself. Sammy is down there, so whoever gets back first go along and make sure he is all right.

'If any of you hear anything, or see anyone, call out.'

Mark seated himself on the chest. 'Leave the lantern here with me, in case there is any trouble,' he said.

The men parted. Crouched in the shadow Jim waited until their footsteps died away. Then he attacked Mark. As with the others his movements were quick, and silent; but even so they were not swift enough. Mark was expecting trouble, and he was prepared for the attack. Together they fought savagely, hitting, kicking, and clawing at one another like two wild beasts. Jim managed to get a stranglehold round Mark's throat, and he held on until he felt his fingers grow numb with exertion. As he flung the semiconscious body of Mark to the ground he could hear footsteps returning. There was not a minute to be lost. Kicking over the lantern, so that the cave was in complete darkness he picked up the chest and staggered towards the tunnel that led back to Mother Redcap's.

His arms ached with the weight of the box, yet he knew he dared not pause for a second. Several times he thought he heard the sound of pursuing footsteps, and tried to increase his pace.

Relief flooded him as he stumbled over Sammy's body. If he had come that far he had only a few more yards to go before he was at the tavern.

He lowered the chest to the ground, and leaning his head against the cold, rough wall. His laboured breathing tore at his chest like a double-edged saw. Now that his task was almost completed he felt too weary even to think. He must get into the tavern before Matt, and his men, caught him. Any minute they might come lumbering up the passage behind him.

He felt the stone panel beneath his fingers, and fumbled with the catch. As the great slab swung inwards he stumbled forward into the room, dragging the box with him. With a final effort he reached up and closed the panel.

The danger was not over. He suspected he was not the only one who knew of the entrance. Matt might know of it, and at any moment might follow him. There was still no time to be lost. Summoning up a reserve of strength, Jim again shouldered the chest, and cautiously made his way up the wide oak staircase making for Melany's room. To his great relief her door was unlocked and swiftly he entered and secured it behind him.

Despite his danger, tenderness flooded his heart as he looked at her as she slept. She made a picture he would not easily forget. Her dark hair framed her face, her red lips were sightly parted, and her long dark lashes curled on her flushed cheeks. She had one bare arm outside the coverlet, and her body rose gently with her deep, regular breathing.

Lowering the chest from his shoulder,

Jim bent over the bed and gently touched one cheek with his lips; she stirred and murmured his name. He was deeply touched. Bending closer he whispered her name, and at the same time gently, but firmly, shaking her by the shoulders.

Her brown eyes opened and stared unseeingly into his.

Then, with a start, she sat bolt upright in bed. He placed his fingers over her mouth in warning.

'Melany, it's urgent. You've got to help me. Where can I hide?'

'But, Jim . . . '

'Quickly, Melany, before Matt and his men get here. Is there any place here, in your room?'

She shook her head, her eyes dark with anguish.

'Are you quite sure? Is there no space at all where you could conceal me for a few hours, until the danger is passed?'

Again she shook her head, and then her face lightened.

'There is a trap door in the floor

under my bed. It's very small, I doubt if you could get into it; and if you were there for any time I am sure you would suffocate.'

Jim was not listening. Already he had dived under the hanging frill of the bed covers and was prising up the boards. Swiftly, he dragged the chest under the bed and lowered it down into the hole. Then he scrabbled in after it.

'Melany?' he called in a low voice. 'Can you hear me?'

'Yes,' came her whisper.

'Stay in your bed, and if anyone comes to your door pretend to be asleep. If they want to come into your room let them. I will stay here under your bed. If anyone does come then I will get into the hole. It will be very cramped, so I will leave the boards open for as long as I can. Don't try to talk to me. Matt, or someone, might creep up and listen at the door and hear us.'

'Very well.'

He heard the bed creak as she re-settled herself, as though for sleep.

Crouched under the bed he listened intently. At any moment now there should be a disturbance below stairs. Matt and his men would return to find the treasure stolen and begin to search the tunnels. They would find the bodies of Mark and Sammy. If Matt knew the secret entrance from the tunnel to the tavern he would be here at any minute.

18

Trembling with fear, at the thought of what might happen if Grenville was discovered in her room, Melany lay listening to the sounds below stairs. They seemed, to her, to have been going on for ever. The heavy hammering on the door was followed by Matt's voice, rough with rage, bellowing, at her aunt to open up.

She could hear their voices growing louder as they came towards the staircase.

'But I tell you we've not seen a creature here this night — not since I bolted and barred the doors round midnight.'

Her aunt's tones were high, and querulous, yet tinged with fear. ' 'Tis wrong of you, Matt, to accuse me of harbouring such a rapscallion. Now that I know him for what he is I'd no more hide him in my house than I would help a customs man. Haven't I always been a good friend to you and you men? You've never known me to hinder you for one minute, nor place any obstacle in your way.'

'Shut your cackling, woman.' Matt's tones were offensive and brutal. 'If you're not hiding the devil then that wench you keep here must be helping him. All I know is that he's battered three of my men insensible, killed young Sammy, and slipped through our fingers with treasure worth a fortune. I intend to search this place, myself, until I find him. And, by God, I'm pretty certain I shall do it.'

She heard her aunt again begin to deny that Grenville had been there, but Matt cut her short with an oath.

'If I have to pull every stone of this place down I'll find where you've hidden him.'

Melany heard sounds of a struggle, followed by a sharp scream from Mother Redcap. She held her breath in terror as heavy footsteps sounded on the stairs. As they reached the top of the staircase she heard Matt detail a man to stand guard.

A cold sweat broke out on her forehead and hands, and for a moment she thought she would swoon as she heard footsteps pause outside her door, and Matt say gruffly, 'I'll handle this.'

Her heart beat madly, pounding within her chest. She buried her face in the pillows to keep herself from screaming as the door burst open and Matt strode into the room.

He crossed to the bed and shook her roughly holding the candle he carried close to her face so that he could look directly into her eyes.

'Speak, wench! Don't stare as if you're moonstruck. I've wasted enough time tonight. Are you hiding Jim Grenville somewhere?'

She tried to answer him, but the words choked in her throat and she made only an inarticulate cry.

Matt turned away in undisguised

scorn. 'You behave like you never entertained a man in bed afore. I warrant if friend Grenville were to appear you'd be quick enough to open your arms to him, not cower under the sheets like a timid virgin.'

The thought seemed suddenly to strike him. 'Maybe that is the cause for your alarm. Maybe the swine is abed with you.'

He surveyed the evenness of the bed which lay undisturbed save where the clothes moulded themselves round the soft curves of her body.

'He takes up precious little room if he is.' He sneered.

Without warning he suddenly swept aside the drapes that hung from the fourposter to the floor and peered underneath them. Melany sank her teeth into her lower lip to prevent herself from screaming out. When he emerged she had control of herself, and her only reaction was a cold reproachful stare.

He stood looking down at her, then

crossed to the built-in closet. Swinging wide the doors he searched inside it, sweeping her gowns unceremoniously to one side.

At last, satisfied that Grenville was not concealed there he made for the door. With his hand on the knob he turned to where she was still half sitting, half lying in her bed; her great dark eyes following his every movement.

Matt returned her gaze with one equally piercing. When he spoke his voice was knife-edged. 'All right, you've won. He's not here but I'd bet a hundred guineas that he's been here tonight, and, what is more, you know where he is at this very minute.'

She held his glance but made no reply.

Matt crossed softly to the bedside.

'Come, Melany, you're a sensible girl, and a pretty one. Don't let your head be turned by any fancy tales he may have told you. You've known me for a long time now, and you know me to be a man as keeps my word.

Help me to find Grenville, and to get back the chest he's stolen from me, and I'll see that you're rewarded handsomely. You'll not need to soil your pretty hands drawing ale for rough sea-men, and fisherfolk; nor waste your nights keeping a bed warm for some rapscallion whose mind is set on someone else. Help me and I'll set you up in a fine house, with a carriage and servants of your own, and not ask a single favour in return, unless you wish to give. Think it over.'

'Get out!' The cold fury of Melany's voice stung like a lash. 'Get out of my room, and buy your favours elsewhere. If there was a man in this house I'd have him thrash you, before he threw you into the river. Get out! Get out before, before . . . ' Her fury choked her, she half rose from the bed, then, conscious that she wore only a nightgown, pulled the counterpane round her in an effort to shield herself from Matt's bold gaze.

His eyes narrowed as he opened the

door behind him.

'Goodnight, Melany! Temper improves your appearance.'

She listened, with strained ears, to the murmur of their voices as Matt and his men took leave of her aunt. As Melany had feared, no sooner had Mother Redcap secured the door behind Matt than she came hurrying upstairs. Putting an arm round Melany's shaking shoulders she tried to comfort her niece.

'There, there! He's gone now. Take no notice of anything he may have said to you. Matt is a rough man when he's roused. Lie down, my dear, and I'll fetch you some warm milk. 'Twill help you to sleep. Lie abed in the morning, this has been a disturbing night, and I know you had soft feelings for Sammy.'

'For Sammy?' Melany looked up startled.

'That fellow Grenville killed him,' Mother Redcap went on. 'Sammy was guarding the passage leading from the caves to here. Three more of Matt's men were attacked as well.'

She shook her head in a puzzled manner. 'I'm wondering if Matt is after the right man. The fellow who was here, that you nursed back to health, looked too pulled down by sickness to have the strength for such goings on.'

Melany made no reply, nor did she try to explain to her aunt that her tears were not for Sammy. She had managed to control herself by the time her aunt returned with the warmed milk.

She murmured her thanks, adding that her head was throbbing wildly and that she would try and sleep as soon as she had drunk it. 'First though,' she insisted, 'I must lock and barricade my door against any chance of Matt returning.'

Mother Redcap smiled, chiding Melany for her silliness.

'It's the only way I will know peace of mind,' Melany insisted.

19

As soon as her aunt left her, Melany locked and barricaded the bedroom door, then swept aside the bed drapes and crawling underneath tapped on the loose floorboards beneath the centre of the bed. At first there was no reply. For one dreadful moment she thought that perhaps Jim Grenville had suffocated.

Slowly the board began to lift upward. With eager fingers she pulled at it.

Grenville's face was wet with sweat, his hair matted and his breathing laboured.

'Another few minutes,' he gasped, 'and . . . '

'Hush!' she laid a hand over his lips, deadening the rest of his sentence.

Already Melany was beginning to gasp for air, in the closeness of the shrouded enclosure underneath the bed.

As she helped Jim to his feet he fell across the bed in a state of complete exhaustion. Gently, Melany slipped a pillow under his head. Crossing to the washstand she dipped a cloth in the earthenware pitcher of water, and dabbed tenderly at his face, and brow. The cold water revived him almost instantaneously. As soon as he was in a sitting position she handed him the glass of warm milk, her aunt had brought for her. He drank greedily then lay back on the pillows exhausted. Tenderly she bathed away the dust and grime, and tried to clean the cuts and scratches about his face, concerned by how pale, and weak, he looked. Dark shadows beneath his eyes told of the strain, and fatigue, he had suffered during the last few days. She sat by his side, stroking his head, until he slept.

The hours slipped by until the pale fingers of dawn parted the curtains, threatening the secret of Melany's room. Panic filled her. If Matt had left a guard outside the house there was now no chance of Jim escaping.

She crept to the window. The dawn showed her a still, and sleeping world. The sands still dappled from the receding tide, were wet and silvery in the early morning light. A few grey gulls circled and swooped over the shore. Satisfied that the house was not being watched she steeled herself to waken Jim.

He awoke groaning. His cuts and bruises from the previous night had become sore and stiff. Gently Melany shook him, and at the same time held a warning hand over his mouth. Immediately he was alert.

'You should have wakened me sooner,' he admonished her in a whisper, when he saw how light the sky had grown.

'What are your plans? What will you do?' she asked urgently.

He rumpled his auburn hair in a worried manner. 'God knows. I've slept when I should have been planning. It is impossible to stay here. If I had

had to stay hidden under your bed much longer last night I should have suffocated.'

'You could leave the chest there,' she suggested.

His eyes narrowed. 'Yes,' he said thoughtfully. 'I suppose I have no alternative. It will be hazardous enough to make my escape, without being hampered by that. The trouble is how can I be sure it will be safe. Matt will stop at nothing to find it.'

Melany looked steadily into his eyes. 'Do you mean to restore it to Cornelius Tobin?'

Jim nodded. 'It will help to recompense him for the loss of the *Golden Lady*. First I must contact him. I must cross to Liverpool without encountering Matt or any of his men . . . '

Melany nodded. The thought that the chest, crammed with treasure, was to remain under the floorboards beneath her bed, filled her with a sickening dread.

Matt was desperate and would stop at nothing. If he suspected that the box was hidden in her room he might even kill her, in order to regain it. Her great love for Jim overcame her fears. She managed a smile as she said, 'The box will be quite safe here, Jim.'

He frowned. 'Don't go letting your aunt, or anyone, think that there is anything hidden in this room. Carry on as normal. If by chance your aunt, or Matt, should find the box, all you have to do is to disclaim all knowledge of it.'

She nodded. 'And when shall I expect to hear from you?'

He looked gloomy and worried as he answered. 'Give me a week. If in that time I have not returned to claim the box you can give me up as dead.'

'And then . . . ?' her voice shook with suppressed emotion.

'You must do as you deem wisest,' he said in a low voice. 'The box then becomes your property. You can keep the contents, give them to Matt, or to

Cornelius Tobin, their rightful owner.'

'I see.' She looked straight into his eyes. 'Then if it should happen that I hear nothing from you during the next week — but pray God it doesn't — I'll see that the task you're setting yourself is completed.'

'You mean . . . ?'

'I will contact Cornelius Tobin, and tell him that it was your wish that the chest should be handed over to him.'

Grenville gathered Melany into his arms. 'Someday, God willing, I'll repay you for all you've done for me. I'll see that you want for nothing. I'll take you away from all this drudgery. You shall have your own carriage, servants to wait on you, and everything you can possibly desire.'

He paused, and looked down at her in surprise, as an hysterical sob escaped her.

'Those are the same things Matt promised me if I would help him to find you and the treasure.'

They looked into each other's eyes

then his arms tightened around her, his lips on hers.

After he released her and crept away, boots in hand, she stood motionless, too scared for his safety to move lest she disturbed her aunt.

20

The library, of St. Hilary's vicarage, was a noble room. Lofty, spacious, and panelled in dark oak, it was essentially a man's room. Bookcases lined three of the walls, the remaining wall was dominated by an imposing stone fire-place. The room's furnishings were equally impressive. Leather armchairs with bulbous carved legs, and arms, stood either side of the great hearth. At the other end of the room a straight-backed leather chair was placed at the handsome carved oak desk. The rich turkey red carpet was matched by heavy, red velvet curtains that swept down to the floor in gracious folds.

The bookcases either side of the window contained mostly religious and reference works such as one would expect to find in the library of a man of God. The cases along the remaining two walls were filled with books of diverse titles, books that had the appearance of being well read.

An oil lamp, standing on the desk, threw a golden gleam over the papers lying in neat piles. It also cast an aura of mellow light round the room nearby, mingling with the dancing firelight, as flames choked, and spluttered, over a huge pine log. The rest of the room was in shadow.

Standing near the fireplace, his legs apart and his head slightly inclined was Matt. The vicar, dwarfed by Matt's bulk, was striding to and fro, his hands clenched behind his back, in the manner of a man grappling with some great problem.

He was a slightly-built man, fair haired, like his cousin Lord Pendleton, and possessing the same cold, penetrating green eyes. His receding chin and thin mouth gave him a sharp cunning appearance. He wore dark knee breeches and a severe black velvet coat, which was buttoned to the neck and devoid of trimmings. His high forehead was puckered and creased by thought as if he were grappling with his sermon for the morrow. Yet such a task he could toss off in the matter of minutes. Seated at the great oak desk, his quill pen between his fingers, his shelves of reference books at hand, he could write a sermon, with ease, in the hour between dinner and supper. The problem which troubled him now was of a much more serious nature.

Pausing in his pacings he swung round suddenly on his heel. Staring up into Matt's dark, swarthy face he almost choked on the words, as in tones of fury, he shouted, 'You're a failure. Understand! A complete failure.'

Matt opened his mouth to defend himself, then shrugged his massive shoulders resignedly.

'Well, aren't you going to say anything?'

Towering over the slight figure of the vicar, Matt shook his head not uttering a word in his own defence. If the gang he controlled with a hand of iron could see him now, he thought, his power over them would be at an end.

Receiving no reply the vicar turned away and resumed his nervous pacing.

'What my cousin Pendleton will say, when the news reaches him, I have no conception. He set great store by your ability to see this affair through successfully.'

'This is the first failure I've ever had,' Matt spoke shortly, and gruffly. He felt aggrieved by the vicar's manner.

'I know that the circumstances leading up to this loss are, according to your tale, so unprecedented in your career of wrecking and smuggling, that you feel some dispensation should be granted. All you had to do,' the vicar had worked himself into a storming rage, 'was to carry a box from here to a boat waiting by the Yellow Noses, and travel with it to Liverpool. There, at the quayside, you would be met by a closed carriage. Along with the chest, you were to be taken to my cousin,

Lord Pendleton. Nothing could have been simpler. Once you had handed the box over to him personally your duties were finished. All that remained was for you to call here, in a month's time, collect the reward and pay your men off. Nothing could have been easier.'

'But how was I to know that someone else knew of your plans for this night?'

The vicar shrugged. 'It was for you to take the necessary precautions. You should be well schooled in these matters by now, you should not require my guidance.'

Matt became surly. 'I had men posted at every entrance as well as those with me when we ran into trouble.'

'And yet you couldn't overcome one man,' sneered the vicar.

Matt groaned. 'Damn it, I didn't know at the time that he was working alone, did I?'

'Oh, of course not,' the vicar's voice was dangerously soft. 'That was why you left the chest unguarded, in the middle of the caves, and were surprised when it vanished.'

'That's not true. Mark was left to guard the chest. When we got back he had been attacked and left senseless on the ground. That's God's truth!'

'God's truth! I wonder if it is even your truth of the tale. How am I to know that this has not been a put-up job, by you and your men, to obtain the treasure for yourselves.'

Matt looked scornful. 'And kill off Sammy, and injure three others of my men, just to prove my story.'

The vicar came closer, and his eyes narrowed as he stared up into Matt's face. 'The loss of the treasure is disastrous. I know that the events you describe make it seem an accident that our plans went awry. The truth is Matt that neither Lord Pendleton nor I trust you. I think you would be capable of any evil deed to justify your own ends. Whatever account you care to give the fact remains that the chest has vanished.'

'Lord Pendleton knows that Grenville is still alive,' Matt argued. Didn't he himself visit here, not many days past, seeking him out.'

'Yes,' the vicar rejoined softly, 'and all because of a tale carried over the water to him by the wench from Mother Redcap's tavern. For all he, or I, know the wench may be in league with you.'

'You give me credit for some careful scheming. Such well laid plans would be beyond my making.'

'Ah, of course, I forgot. You are incapable of planning even a simple thing — like the carrying of a chest from one point to another, when every entrance is well guarded.'

For a moment it looked as though Matt would strike the man, who stood there tormenting him in a thin cold voice. His massive fist clenched, and unclenched, trying to control the fury that was welling up inside him.

'Talking with you is useless,' he snarled. 'I'll wait until Lord Pendleton arrives. He at least might believe an honest tale when he hears one.'

'Judging from the noise in the hall you have no need to wait any longer. This will be my cousin now. I trust your story will ring more pleasantly in his ears than it does in mine.'

As he spoke the door swung open, and Pendleton, his face ablaze with fury, strode into the room.

'What goddamn nonsense is this message,' he railed. 'Do you take me for a fool? Am I to believe that the chest we guarded so carefully, all these past weeks, has vanished?'

'That is what Matt here would have us believe, cousin.'

Pendleton swung round to face Matt.

'Come man,' he ordered, 'speak up and let's hear your report. By God! You'd better make it convincing.'

'He'll make it good. He's practised it on me. Will you take a drink, cousin? It might help to make Matt's tale more credible.'

21

Long after Matt had been dismissed from their presence Pendleton and his cousin sat in the massive leather armchairs before the blazing log fire, sipping their glasses of rum, and gloomily debating the next course of action open to them.

'You know, Will,' the vicar said, as he filled his deep bowled pipe, 'I think perhaps we were too hard with Matt. After all, this fellow Grenville must be a wily bird. This is the second time he's managed to escape us.'

'There won't be a third time,' grumbled Pendleton, bitterly. 'Next time I'll handle the matter personally.'

'And by that do you mean you think I've failed?'

'I mean, Japhet, just whatever you think I mean. Damn it man, I made no reproach the first time this fellow slipped through our clutches. Anyone could have struck a man down, and taken him for dead, at a time like that. I don't blame Matt, or you either, that the sea washed him back high and dry onto the shore. That was just ill luck; but when a plan as carefully laid as ours was tonight is foiled it means that somebody hasn't played their part.'

'But you heard what Matt had to say. The plans were carried out to the letter. Every man was at his post; the chest was well guarded . . . '

'And still,' interrupted Pendleton, scornfully, 'they failed even though they were using a network of caves, with every exit guarded.'

The vicar blew out a cloud of smoke, and gazed contemplatively, as it soared in a bluish grey screen between him and the fire. 'You heard Matt's story.'

Will Pendleton's eyes narrowed. 'Yes, I heard Matt's story, and I can't help wondering. No one at Mother Redcap's has seen Grenville since the night Matt sent him to the Ring o' Bells.'

The vicar laughed shortly. 'Well?'

'If that story is correct was it Grenville who attacked Matt, and his men, tonight.'

'Who knows the true value of the contents of that chest?'

'Apart from Grenville, only Matt, you or I.' Pendleton answered.

'I was over on the Liverpool side waiting for Matt to come over by boat,' he added. 'Your men found me still waiting there when they came to tell me the news.'

'So what?'

Pendleton remained silent for several minutes. A sneering smile played round the corners of his thin mouth.

'Well, it means that only you, or Matt, could have spirited away the chest.'

The vicar sat bolt upright in his chair and angrily faced his cousin. 'That's a foul accusation to make. I've helped you through a good many deals, have you ever known me to play false in any of them? I've seen you've had your fair share regardless of whether you took an equal part of the risk, or not. The time has come, I can see, when we take a reckoning of the whole matter. I've been pretty dissatisfied with the arrangements for some time now. I do all the organising and take most of the risks.'

Pendleton's eyes blazed with anger. 'So you are dissatisfied.' His voice was dangerously calm. 'You may do the arranging; act as an intermediary between Matt and his men, I don't deny you do. I don't repudiate either that it's your cloth that keeps you above suspicion with the customs men. No one would think of disturbing the sanctity of a church when they're looking for rum, and bales of silk, and cotton, or tobacco, that have disappeared from a wreck. No one would dream of opening up family vaults. If you are seen talking to the likes of Matt it is assumed that the good vicar is merely trying to save the feeble sinner. Little do people suspect that he is planning another wreck, or conveying information about the disposal of contraband goods.

No, cousin, I must grant that you have your uses, but to what avail if you did not receive the vital information concerning the cargo aboard every vessel which enters the Mersey. To lie in wait, night after night, and to wreck all, and every, ship that entered the Mersey would be a profitless task. Negro slaves might fetch a goodly price in Liverpool, but as smuggled wares they would prove mighty troublesome.

It is the information I provide you with, which makes the venture profitable. You may think you take all the risk but believe me you are nothing but a pawn in this game. If anyone takes risks I do. If it was suspected for one moment that I passed on the confidential knowledge which I glean over morning coffee, or an evening dinner, to the likes of Matt, and his men, some of the less fortunate ship-owners would kill me with their own bare hands. If Cornelius Tobin knew, why where then would I be?'

'Probably denied his house and the privilege of dancing attention on his daughter. All right, cousin, we'll agree you take an equal share of the danger. The truth is we're all in this together, and if one man should ever squeal, then the whole lot of us would swing. I doubt if either my cloth, or your title, would stand us in any stead then.'

'No, you're probably right.'

A silence fell between them. The fire crackled, and sent a shower of small sparks up the wide chimney, igniting the furry top layer of soot until it sparkled like stars.

'And you think that Matt is to be trusted?' asked Pendleton, at length.

'I think so. There were too many men with him for him to try to trick us.'

'Unless he had bribed them to help him.'

The vicar shook his head. 'It's unlikely. Matt is a wily fellow. He knows how difficult it would be to dispose of the stuff. No, all Matt wanted was to get his hands on his share of the spoils, and pay his men off. They've never had to wait as long as this before, and they were growing restless.'

'Do you think then that some of them may have banded together to steal the chest?'

The vicar shook his head.

'Well then,' Pendleton smote his knee with a clenched fist, 'What the hell do you think?'

The vicar smoothed his clean-shaven chin thoughtfully, running his long sensitive fingers over it in a gently massaging manner.

'I think,' he said at length, 'that the girl at Mother Redcap's is lying. I think she knows where Grenville is.'

'Go on!'

The vicar shrugged. 'It's purely conjecture, dear cousin. My guess is that she learned when the chest was to be moved and told Grenville.'

Pendleton rose angrily from his chair. 'You've sat there half the night, knowing this yet saying nothing. We should have gone there immediately, and searched the tavern, questioned the wench, and the old woman. I warrant the place is full of nooks and crannies they could hide a man in.'

'Calm yourself, cousin. The night has not been wasted. I sent Matt there after you dismissed him so abruptly. By now, he should have made his search, and will be here any moment to report.'

22

Corrina was haunted by a desire to see Grenville. Ever since Melany's visit to Liverpool she had been remembering odd details of his appearance, and mannerisms, that she had long forgotten, and had been mentally comparing him with Lord Pendleton. She felt certain that any day now Lord Pendleton would propose to her, and before she accepted him she wanted to be sure that Grenville was completely out of her mind and her heart.

For the first few months after Grenville had left in the *Golden Lady* she had thought of him every night. Gradually her memories had faded and her heart no longer fluttered like a trapped butterfly whenever the sun caught the glint of auburn hair. She no longer spent long hours on her knees praying for his safety and the speedy return of the *Golden Lady*.

After Lord Pendleton had come into her life, bringing a whirl of gaiety and excitement, Grenville had become just a dream.

It had been a shock to learn that the *Golden Lady* had been wrecked and plundered only the other side of the river. When her father had told her that the *Golden Lady* was due in at any time, she recalled telling Lord Pendleton the news, trying to invest in him some of her own excitement about the treasure that might be aboard when she docked.

Surely, she thought, had she had any feeling for Grenville then would she have told Lord Pendleton, who was his rival, of the *Golden Lady*'s homecoming. It was only after the wench from Mother Redcap's had brought her the message that Jim Grenville was alive that she had begun to feel a re-awakening of her love for him.

Many times in the past weeks she

wished that she had told her father about the girl's visit. It had been Pendleton's idea that the girl was probably only spinning a tale hoping for a reward, that held her back.

She had been surprised when, a few weeks later, Pendleton had taken her to Mother Redcap's tavern, to see if there was any further news of Grenville.

Looking back on the events of that day Corrina shivered with fear. Melany had seemed very taken aback at seeing them and Grenville was nowhere to be found. True, Mother Redcap had appeared to corroborate Melany's story. They had gone on to visit the vicar of St. Hilary's, whom Pendleton claimed was his cousin. Corrina shuddered at the memory of the strange pale-faced man who had regarded her so coldly, and who had conversed in subtle riddles, quite beyond her understanding.

The bleakness of the countryside had made her blood run chill. There was something evil, and sinister, about the whole place. On impulse she resolved to seek out Melany, and question her about Grenville's whereabouts.

She could take Nabob. Their coachman was a stout fellow. She would take him into her confidence and he would see she came to no harm.

She would tell her father that she had heard of a woman living in Wallasey who was a remarkably fine needlewoman.

'And you are willing to journey over the river just to meet such a woman?' Cornelius Tobin's eyes twinkled kindly at his daughter over the breakfast table. 'It must be some wondrous special work you wish to have done. Something very intricate. Something for some outstanding event maybe?' Although his eyes were laughing his tones were serious.

She smiled coyly at his teasing. If he liked to think she was contemplating marriage she would not spoil his fun.

If her journey was successful, and she learnt the whereabouts of Grenville, it might help her father recover the treasure chest that had been stolen from the *Golden Lady* when she was wrecked. Although he had not spoken of it to her she knew that in his heart he was bitter about the entire affair.

If Grenville had returned with the treasure, and brought the *Golden Lady* safely to port, the rejoicings would have been tumultuous.

Melany was hanging out clothes in the small yard at the back of the tavern. Chickens scratched by her feet and a half wild, ginger cat crouched on an upturned barrel watching the world with narrowed green eyes.

She heard a coach drive up and answered her aunt's call to find Corrina Tobin framed in the doorway.

Melany's first thoughts were that Jim Grenville had reached Liverpool safely and that Corrina had come to bring her news of him and to collect the chest. Her worries over Jim's safety were dulled by the constant burden of the secret she guarded in her bedroom.

Every night she set her mind at rest that the chest was still hidden in the recess beneath her bed.

Her warm greeting was from her heart. Her relief was so great that she failed to notice the look of surprise on Mother Redcap's face.

Melany broke the uneasy silence. 'Perhaps you would care for some refreshment, Miss Tobin. You must feel fatigued after your long journey.'

Corrina acquiesced.

'I'll fetch a glass of wine for you then I must about my business,' Mother Redcap offered.

'You are very kind,' Corrina said graciously.

As soon as Mother Redcap left them Melany asked, 'Why have you come? Speak quickly, while we are alone.'

Corrina took a deep breath. 'I have something to tell you, something you won't like.'

'Well,' Melany's small white teeth caught at her under-lip as she steeled herself to hear Corrina's news.

'Many weeks ago you asked me to deliver a message from Jim Grenville to my father.'

'Well?'

'I didn't deliver your message. I put the matter from my mind. I would probably never have thought of it again had not Lord Pendleton suggested we should pay Grenville a visit.'

'I remember.'

'Did you tell Grenville of our visit?'

'Why do you ask?'

Corrina sighed. 'He has made no attempt to contact me or my father . . . '

'You mean . . . ' Melany's eyes were wide and worried. 'You mean you've not heard from him at all. Not even during these past few days?'

Corrina shook her head.

'You're quite certain. Perhaps your father has had some news from him.'

'Not to my knowledge. I'm quite sure that if he had done he would have mentioned it. He knows I hold Captain Grenville in high esteem.'

Melany allowed the reference to

Corrina's hold over Grenville's affections to pass unnoticed. Her face was ashen as she repeated in a half whisper, 'And you've not heard or seen anything of him in the last few days.'

'You seem to think we should have done.'

Melany looked deliberately over Corrina's fashionable figure, as if weighing up her true value. Then staring into the china blue eyes she said, 'How far can I trust you?'

For a moment she thought Corrina was going to slap her face. Two high spots of colour shone through the careful powdering.

'I may have deceived you in the past, but believe me I am more than anxious now to see Captain Jim Grenville. It is my wish to see him again and test our feelings for each other.'

'Very well.' Melany's tones were cold. 'A few nights ago, Jim Grenville tricked the wreckers who attacked the *Golden Lady*, and retrieved the chest of treasure. Matt and his men are searching for him. He left here, several nights ago, to come to Liverpool, to seek out your father, and tell him the entire story and obtain his help. I thought you were bringing a message to say he had reached the shelter of your house and safety.'

23

For a day and a night Jim Grenville hid near the quayside at Seacombe. The journey from Mother Redcap's had been uneventful. It seemed, that for the present, Matt's men had given up the chase.

He had hoped to slip aboard a small fishing boat at Seacombe and then under cover of darkness sail across the Mersey to Liverpool. But there were no small craft moored at the quayside, only a few ferry boats waiting for their passengers.

He spent the first day hiding in an old disused barn, some half mile or so from the river front. He slept fitfully and awoke at nightfall cold, stiff and hungry and returned to the riverside. He must at all costs cross the river before day-break he decided. He planned to hide on one of the larger ferrying boats and trust to luck that he would be able to slip ashore undetected when they reached Liverpool.

He studied the boats as they pulled in to the quayside. For a long time he saw nothing that suited his purpose. For the most part the boats were too small. Even if he did manage to slip on board unnoticed there would be nowhere to hide.

He was almost in despair when towards midnight a boat much larger than any of the others pulled into the side and as the gangplank was lowered a horse and rider came ashore led by a servant who held the animal by it's bridle, 'I'll not be more than an hour at the outside. Wait here and keep the boat ready. Understand?'

'Very good, my Lord.' The servant handed over the reins and stepped back.

As soon as the clatter of the horses hooves died away the servant turned to the waiting boatman.

'You heard that, Jimmy? My Lord Pendleton will return within the hour. What say you we refresh ourselves down below in that cosy little cabin of yours, and await his pleasure.'

The boatman gave a deep laugh. 'As you will.' He took the pipe from his mouth and spat into the dark waters, then turned and led the way down to his cabin.

Hardly able to contain his excitement Jim waited a few minutes to give them time to settle over their rum and pipes; then swiftly, but as quietly as he could, slipped on deck.

The boat was small and he wondered where he should hide.

Before he could find a suitable niche he heard the sound of footsteps. The boat owner was coming up on deck.

Grenville looked swiftly round him. There was nowhere he could hide and it was useless to try and get ashore again without arousing suspicion. Taking courage he walked boldly up to the man, meeting him as soon as his head and shoulders appeared above the hatchway.

'Are you the owner of this boat?' he demanded. 'I wish to speak with Lord Pendleton, and I understand he is on board.'

'No, not he, Sir,' the man spoke slowly, trying to get a look at Grenville in the light of the lantern he carried.

'Then I've been misinformed.' Grenville turned away. 'I've mistaken the boat no doubt.'

As he would have started down the gang plank the man laid a hand on his arm. 'Just a minute. Lord Pendleton will be returning within the hour. He has just ridden off to visit his cousin at Wallasey,' the man went on. 'He said he wouldn't be long and bid me wait his return. His man is below, shall I get him?'

Jim thought for a moment. If the fellow went below to call Pendleton's manservant he would have an opportunity to slip ashore.

'Yes,' he said, 'fetch Lord Pendleton's

man. I'll have a word with him. Perhaps he can tell me how long his master will be away, and whether it is worth my while to wait for him.'

'Very good.'

Crossing to the companionway the sailor bellowed down, 'Thomas Goodman, you're wanted aboard.'

Silently Grenville cursed the fellow. He had counted on him going below to give the message. While he was still on deck there was no possible chance of escape.

As Goodman appeared Grenville determined to brazen the matter out.

'You are Lord Pendleton's servant?' he asked, studying the livery the man wore.

The man stared boldly at him, as if trying to remember who he might be. 'He said he would be back within the hour,' he said slowly, at length. 'I didn't catch your name.'

'I didn't give you my name. I'll wait for your master, the matter I wish to discuss with him is of a private nature.'

'As you like,' Goodman gave a slight shrug and made as if to retire. He exchanged a significant glance with the owner of the boat and then said, 'We were partaking of some refreshment, below deck, perhaps you would care for a glass. Would help keep the cold of the night air out of your bones.'

'Very well!' Grenville tried not to sound eager. It was many hours since he had tasted food or drink and he was both ravenously hungry and parched with thirst.

Feeling more like a prisoner than a guest Grenville passed an hour with the two men. It was with a mixture of relief and despair that he finally heard the sound of horses hooves ring out.

'Here's his Lordship now, Sir. I'll tell him you're waiting to speak with him.'

Left alone in the cabin Grenville looked round for means of escape in vain. His heart beat faster with an increased sense of dread as he heard the sound of footsteps descending the companionway.

As a handsomely dressed man stepped into full view he stood up and asked, 'Lord Pendleton?'

24

Corrina rose from her dressing-table and surveyed herself in the long mirror with a satisfied smile.

She was not too sure what Lord Pendleton had meant by his strange message but she sensed that tonight was to be a very special occasion.

His note, brought by a servant, had read,

> 'Tonight, at 7 o'clock my carriage will call for you, and I trust you will honour me with your company at dinner. Believe me, my dear Corrina, it will be a night you will long remember.
>
> Your humble servant,
>
> PENDLETON

She had chosen a gown of shimmering, ice blue silk, that matched her eyes.

It was cut in a low curve at the neck, the tight fitting bodice revealing the ripeness of her breasts, the skirt a billowing mass of rustling silk. Around her throat an immense sapphire sparkled and gleamed on its fine gold chain. She wore no other jewellery but instead had dressed her hair in low ringlets which cascaded like golden drops around her tiny ears.

Slipping a white fur cape around her shoulders she stood by the window waiting for Pendleton's carriage.

As it swept up the drive she took a last look at her reflection. Nabob stood waiting at the foot of the wide staircase. He wore a pale blue satin jerkin over rich plum-coloured trousers. He bowed almost to the ground as she descended the stairs and then fell into step behind her as she walked to the carriage.

As the door slammed behind them, and the horses responded to the lash of the coachman's whip, she was aware of a feeling of anticipation.

She had spoken to her father about

the visit but he had not been pleased that she had been invited alone.

'It's not fitting for a young lady to be travelling alone through the streets at night,' he grumbled. 'If the fellow wants your company he should call for you or invite some member of your family to accompany you.'

'He knows Nabob will accompany me.'

'Nabob!' Her father spoke contemptuously. He had no time for the blackamoor whom he considered a dressed-up doll; a foolish fancy of the age and one to which his daughter was pandering.

'Perhaps Lord Pendleton's real reason for sending for me in this manner is that he has something private and personal to ask me.'

Cornelius Tobin remained silent. At length he said, 'Well, if he has I hope you give careful consideration to your answer. I have long been expecting him to approach me to know if he might ask you to become his wife, and I've looked forward to the day with mixed feelings. 'Twould be a fine match but not if it meant going against the feelings of your own heart. Do you love the fellow, Corrina? Be honest with me now. It's the truth I want to hear from you.'

Corrina's reply was guarded. 'There is no one else with whom I spend so much of my time.'

Her father regarded her shrewdly but made no further comment.

Now, in Pendleton's carriage and on her way to his house, Corrina wondered what answer she should give Lord Pendleton if he proposed to her.

Pendleton was waiting on the steps as the carriage swept up the wide curving drive. Brushing aside the liveried footman he opened the carriage door and helped her to alight.

Holding both her hands he led her into the great entrance hall and then stepping back a pace surveyed her appraisingly.

'A dream! A vision!' he enthused, as his eyes swept over her. 'But come,' he lifted her fur cape from her shoulders and dropping it into a chair swept her forward towards the library door. 'In here is someone who will revel in the sight of your beauty and radiance.'

He pushed open the heavy oak door. The massive book-lined room was dimly lit and for a moment, after the brightness of the hall, she could see no one. From a deep armchair a figure rose. A man with a shock of fiery auburn hair came forward with hands outstretched. A voice she remembered from the past said, 'Corrina!' and she found herself looking into the grey eyes of Jim Grenville.

In an amused voice Pendleton said, 'My dear Corrina, have you no word of welcome for the Captain?'

'I'm sorry,' her voice sounded strange and high pitched in her ears. She held out her hands to Jim, 'I heard you were lost at sea . . . killed by wreckers who plundered the *Golden Lady*.'

Grenville spoke with restraint. 'As

you can see I was fortunate enough to escape.'

'Come,' Pendleton broke in, 'we can talk about these things over the wine and food that awaits us. I warrant you will have many a saucy story to tell us of the wench at Mother Redcap's who nursed you and hid you all these weeks. Did you not say you hid in her bedchamber the entire time?'

Grenville's eyes darkened with anger but his voice was carefully controlled as he replied, 'No, merely in the same house. Melany was kindness itself. An escaped man runs the risk of finding few who will befriend him.'

'Especially in such a lawless place as Wallasey. My cousin is the vicar there you know. He has a most unrewarding and thankless task trying to preach the word of God to such people. Those that listen are too ignorant to understand him, and those who have brains enough to understand him prefer to devote their time to other pursuits. A wild and unkempt lot, so he tells me.

We shall be able to enjoy a first hand account from you, Captain Grenville.'

'I'm afraid that apart from Mother Redcap and her niece, Melany, I met few people though I agree with you it's very bleak and wild.'

'True, true.' Pendleton agreed. 'Why even we thought that it was desolate when we visited my cousin, some few weeks ago, didn't we, Corrina.'

She waited for him to continue, to explain to Grenville why they had made that journey. She was filled with a sense of foreboding at the meeting of these two men.

She could not understand how Jim Grenville came to be in Pendleton's house. She recalled her recent conversation with Melany who had said that Jim was on his way to Liverpool to tell her father how the *Golden Lady* had been wrecked and how he had escaped and had recovered the treasure from the wreckers. So what was he doing here, in Pendleton's house, when he should have been with her father. Again and again the question pounded her brain while dinner was being served and they talked of general matters.

As soon as the meal was over Pendleton suggested they should retire to the drawing-room, where, if Corrina expressed no objection, they might enjoy their port and cigars in her company.

Pendleton kept a firm hold on Corrina's arm as he escorted her from one room to the other. She sensed his reluctance that she should be in Jim's company alone for even the fraction of a second.

When they were seated in the elaborately furnished drawing-room with its heavy tapestries and rich satin and velvet hangings, Corrina said casually, 'My father will be overjoyed to hear of your safety and anxious to talk with you.'

Before Jim could reply Pendleton said, in dangerously smooth tones, 'Captain Grenville is my guest, my dear. For the present I think a period of complete rest is necessary for him. He has had some arduous experiences. I refuse to let him leave here until he is stronger.'

Grenville leaned forward in his chair. 'I appreciate your kindness, and concern, but already I feel stronger. I think I should call on Cornelius Tobin as soon as possible.'

'As soon as you are fit enough to stand the strain of such a meeting,' returned Pendleton evenly. 'Consider the matter carefully, dear Captain. You can hardly expect Cornelius Tobin to welcome you when you have lost both the ship he prized and the treasure she carried. When you are fully recovered, and not until then, Corrina will acquaint her father of your arrival in Liverpool, and arrange a meeting.'

'Come,' he seized a bottle and filled three glasses. 'Let us drink a toast to our future, may we all prosper and achieve our ambitions.'

25

Cornelius Tobin's face was stern at breakfast the next morning when Corrina told him of her visit to Lord Pendleton's, and that Jim Grenville had been there.

'Why did you not tell me of Grenville's escape earlier, my dear?'

Corrina shook her head. She looked pale and listless with dark smudges beneath her eyes and Tobin's heart was stirred by her apparent distress.

'I had every intention of giving you the message when the girl from Mother Redcap's brought it but in the excitement of acquiring Nabob I forgot it. It was only later, when Lord Pendleton took me over to Wallasey to visit his cousin, the vicar of St. Hilary's, and we called at Mother Redcap's to see if Grenville was still there, that I remembered I hadn't told you. Since Grenville wasn't there and you appeared to have put the loss of the *Golden Lady* from your mind, I thought it wisest not to speak about it.'

'And yet you mention it now.'

'Well, now everything is so different. Until last night I had no actual proof that Jim Grenville was alive.'

'But surely you were able to tell from the girl's description of the man she had nursed back to health whether or not it was Jim Grenville. You knew him well enough before he sailed.'

'Melany never described the man she was sheltering and I never questioned her about him.'

Tobin shook his head in bewilderment. Corrina's story seemed wildly improbable. Almost three months had passed since the *Golden Lady* had been wrecked. During that time those bodies which had been washed up had long since been buried. There had been no trace of the treasure. Grenville's body had never been found but that had not been proof that he was still alive.

'Well,' he said at length, 'assuming that Grenville is alive and that you saw him last night, what is your next step?'

Corrina shook her head. 'I had the strange feeling that Lord Pendleton was holding him a prisoner.'

'A prisoner! But that is utter nonsense!' Cornelius Tobin mopped at his florid face with a square of spotless white lawn as he paced to and fro agitatedly. 'I shall go to Lord Pendleton's immediately and seek out Grenville and listen to his version of this strange turn of events.'

Corrina shook her head again. 'That would be no good. Lord Pendleton would not leave you alone with him so it would be impossible to learn the real truth. Oh, father,' Corrina clung to Tobin and buried her head on his breast. 'We must do something, I love Jim Grenville. I have tried so hard to forget him. I thought it would be such a fine thing to be Lady Pendleton. Now . . . now when I have seen them together I know in my heart that it is Jim Grenville I love. I tried so hard to forget him. Possibly it was because I didn't want to believe he was still alive that I acted as I did forgetting to tell you about Melany's visit.'

At a loss for words Tobin stroked his daughter's head in silence. That she should one day marry Grenville had long been his secret wish. When he had heard that the *Golden Lady* had been wrecked his immediate concern had been for Grenville. Now that he had heard from her own lips that she was really in love with Jim Grenville his immediate resolve was to do all within his power to re-unite them.

'Well, my dear,' he stroked the golden hair gently and raising her face looked searchingly into the blue eyes, now dimmed with tears. 'What suggestion have you. Is there anything you would like me to do.'

Corrina nodded. 'Yes, father. I want us to go across to Wallasey and seek out Melany and find out if she knows what Jim is doing at Lord Pendleton's house.'

Tobin was about to demur. He had many important appointments, then seeing the pleading in Corrina's eyes he gave way.

'Very well, my dear. Finish your breakfast. I will ring for the carriage to be prepared.'

Corrina made an effort to complete her meal while Cornelius Tobin paced to and fro, deep in thought, until the carriage was brought to the door. As they descended the steps Corrina suddenly clutched at her father's arm in surprise. Coming towards the house was Melany.

26

Cornelius Tobin and Corrina listened in silence while Melany related all that had happened since the night the *Golden Lady* had been wrecked.

She spoke quickly, hiding nothing except her own feelings for Grenville. She told of how she had failed to contact Tobin so had left a message with Corrina and Lord Pendleton. She related how she had nursed Grenville back to health; of how her aunt had asked Matt, the leader of the wreckers, to take him into service. Corrina's face paled as Melany related how Grenville had taken the perilous journey over the Bidston Moss, carrying what he thought to be contraband tobacco.

Tobin's eyes shone with excitement when he heard how Grenville had managed to recover the chest from Matt and his men.

'Do you mean to tell me that the treasure that was aboard the *Golden Lady* is safe?' he asked incredulously.

Melany nodded.

'And you know where it is?'

Again Melany nodded. 'When Jim Grenville left my aunt's tavern to try and get in touch with you he entrusted me with the secret of where he had hidden the chest. He said if I did not hear from him within a week I was to take charge of it.'

'I see.' Tobin rose from his chair and paced the floor.

'I have not seen the contents of the chest but he assured me it contained a king's ransom,' Melany went on. 'He felt it would more than compensate for the loss of the *Golden Lady*.'

'Go on, go on.'

Melany bit her underlip. 'There is something else first.'

Tobin exhaled impatiently. 'What is it, my girl. Is it a reward you are after. If you can return the treasure to me, or tell me how I can find it, I shall reward you generously, never fear.'

Melany drew herself up proudly. 'I am not seeking a reward for myself. In return for the information I can give you I want your solemn oath that you will do everything within your power to help me find Jim Grenville.'

'You mean *you* don't know where he is?' Corrina gasped unbelievingly.

Cornelius Tobin laid a hand on Melany's shoulder. 'You have not wasted your time telling us your story. I am indeed grateful to you for all you've done for Captain Grenville. I can never thank you deeply enough for your courage in coming here and relating the events you have. I am sure it will lighten your mind when I tell you that not an hour before you came I heard of Captain Grenville — the first news I have received of him since the night of the wreck.'

'And he is . . . ?' the words died on Melany's lips.

'Fear not. He is alive, and not

twelve hours ago was dining with my daughter.'

Melany stared unbelievingly from Corrina to her father. The colour drained from her face, her voice was barely a whisper as she said, 'I can't believe it. There must be some mistake. How could he be so cruel as to leave me in suspense like this.'

Corrina rose from her chair and took one of Melany's hands between her own soft white ones.

'You must listen and believe what I am going to tell you. What my father says is true but there is more.'

In a low voice she told of her visit to Lord Pendleton's home and her suspicion that Grenville was being held prisoner there.

Melany stared at her in alarm.

'What are you going to do?'

'We were about to cross to Wallasey, to seek you out and learn what you knew, when you arrived.'

'Can you tell us anything more?' Tobin asked.

Melany did not reply immediately. She looked from Tobin's florid face to Corrina's pale and worried one. 'There is one way we might be able to get the information to him.' Her eyes lit up eagerly as a plan developed in her mind. 'Yes,' she went on enthusiastically. 'I think it might work well.' She turned to Tobin who was watching her keenly. 'First collect the chest and put it somewhere safe. On her next visit to Lord Pendleton's, Corrina must let it be known that the treasure has been restored to you. It may mystify Lord Pendleton, but Grenville will know that I have carried out my promise to him.'

'I think we should do as Melany suggests, father,' pleaded Corrina.

Melany flashed her a grateful look. For a moment she forgot that Corrina was her rival for Jim Grenville's affections. Nothing, it seemed, mattered save that they should outwit the wreckers.

For the next hour they planned and

schemed, until their plan was perfected.

It was agreed that after dark Tobin would cross to Wallasey by boat. He would anchor in the small cove about half a mile down-stream from Red Bett's Pool. Four men would stay guard there while Tobin, and the rest of his men set out for Mother Redcap's. Melany would be waiting for them to show Tobin where the chest was hidden.

'There is a great deal left to chance,' Tobin reflected. 'There is a great deal left to chance. I would prefer to come in daylight with a body of well-armed men capable of dealing with any trouble we're likely to meet.'

'No, you must do this my way,' Melany pleaded. 'Many of the smugglers are my aunt's best customers. If they learnt that she had been concerned in hiding the treasure they would turn against her, even kill her. They are wild, dangerous men and their leader, Matt, would stop at nothing, and would show no mercy for any of us.'

27

For a long time after Melany had left Corrina sat curled up in the window seat staring out with unseeing eyes. She found it a wearisome business trying to organise her muddled thoughts.

Now that she had actually seen Grenville again, and had had the opportunity of comparing him with Pendleton, she was in no doubt as to which man she truly loved. Whether to follow the guidance of her heart, or whether to pander to her ambition to become Lady Pendleton, was the problem that faced her.

She never for one moment doubted that Grenville's affections for her remained the same as they had been before he sailed in the *Golden Lady*. Nor had she any doubts that as soon as a suitable opportunity presented itself Lord Pendleton would propose to her.

An urge to see them both again, to have an opportunity of talking alone with Grenville, seized her.

Within half an hour, accompanied by Nabob, she was on her way to Lord Pendleton's. Throughout the drive Corrina felt her spirits rising at the thought of seeing Jim Grenville again so soon.

If Lord Pendleton was surprised at seeing her he masked it well. He received her in the library and rang for coffee to be served as if the meeting had been of his own arranging.

'I thought you wouldn't be able to keep away for long,' he murmured, as he helped her off with her cloak. 'I do believe it is the hope of seeing Captain Grenville that has brought you out so early in the day.'

Corrina laughed lightly. A feeling of warm elation filled her, she felt too light-hearted to take exception to Pendleton's words. 'Let us say the weather enticed me out,' she said gaily.

He laughed sardonically. 'Do you

want us to drink our coffee alone, or shall we invite Grenville to join us?'

She shrugged delicately. 'As he is your guest it would be hardly fitting to leave him alone, would it?' she replied coyly.

Pendleton made no answer but drew Corrina into his arms, his lips exploring the nape of her neck.

Impatiently she pushed him aside.

'Really! What would we do if Captain Grenville walked in on us.'

Pendleton made no reply. He stood looking down at her in a calculating manner for several seconds. Then, without a word, his arms dropped to his sides and he turned on his heel and walked to the window.

When Grenville entered a few moments later there was an air of discord in the room.

Corrina greeted him warmly, enquiring as to the state of his health, whether he had slept well and whether he felt strong enough to venture out of the house.

Before he could reply Pendleton

swung round, and in a voice calculated to brook no arguing said, 'Captain Grenville will remain here, in my house, until I am perfectly satisfied that he is fully restored to health.'

'You make it sound as though he were your prisoner,' Corrina pouted.

'And perhaps he is,' Pendleton retorted.

The reply stung Corrina to anger. 'What right have you to keep him a prisoner. I believe you are only doing it to torment me.'

Pendleton's eyes held hers as he said, 'And if I am?'

As if a curtain had been pushed aside Corrina saw him for what he was. In a flash she saw what her life would be if she married him. The genteel polished manners and courteous speech masked a cold and calculating mind. To obtain the title 'Lady Pendleton' would not be a bargain for her.

'What do you stand to gain by it,' she asked bitterly.

'That is something both of you are

asking. Something to which I, and I alone, know the answer.'

He turned to Grenville, and said in a taunting tone, 'I am holding you prisoner, at any rate until tonight. Then my cousin, the Vicar of St. Hilary's, will have had a chance of talking with you. It won't be to enquire after the state of your health, or your soul either.'

Corrina's face flushed with temper. 'You're damnable,' she said angrily. 'I long suspected it but this is proof. Melany said she thought you were connected with the wreckers, and now I'm convinced that you are.'

'Melany? Ah, yes! I remember her, the wench at Mother Redcap's tavern. And has she been to see you, to enquire whether her lover, has come sneaking back to you.'

'That'll do, Pendleton.' Jim's tone was icy, and his eyes glinted dangerously. 'Melany has been a true friend to me and I'll not have her name smirched by your foul tongue.'

Pendleton bowed mockingly. 'As you will.' He turned to Corrina. 'I'm afraid, my dear, that you have no choice but to remain faithful to me. Your old love has cast you off and taken up with a serving wench.'

'Your words mean nothing to me,' Corrina told him. 'I am not my father's daughter for nothing. I believe you *are* one of the wreckers who sank and plundered the *Golden Lady*.'

'Come, come.' The words rolled off Pendleton's tongue like pearls off velvet. 'You speak harshly and unimaginatively. Do you really think that I donned fisherman's garb, and took up a club, and lay in wait on some desolate spot on the Wallasey coast?' He held out his hand expressively. 'Do you see the marks of violence on these?'

Corrina knocked them aside contemptuously. 'You have neither the ability nor the courage,' she said scathingly. 'You prefer to spend your nights planning such deeds, either here or in the company of your cousin. Then you hire men, ruffians like that fellow Matt, to do your dirty deeds for you.'

'Melany has told you a great deal. Did she also tell you where the treasure was hidden?'

Triumphantly Corrina flung at him, 'The chest will be safely in my father's possession after tonight. You and your cousin, and the band of cut-throats you hire, have lost all claims to it.'

'Stop! Corrina, stop!' Too late Grenville foresaw what she was telling Lord Pendleton.

As she turned and saw his stricken face and Lord Pendleton's self-satisfied smirk she realised that she had given Pendleton the very information he had been trying to obtain.

'Oh, Jim,' she flung herself into Grenville's arms. 'What have I said, what have I done. Have I spoiled all Melany's plans for tonight.'

'Hush! Hush!' Grenville clapped a hand over her mouth.

Pendleton stood with feet apart, arms folded over his chest, a malicious smirk twisting his mouth. 'Well, Captain,' he announced, 'I will leave you two to enjoy one another's company while I go and make ready to intercept the plans laid for tonight.' As he strode to the door Corrina pulled herself from Jim's arms and rushed forward.

Turning, Pendleton pushed her roughly backwards.

'You will stay here. Make no mistake, you cannot escape. I will send a message home by your coachman that will satisfy your father.'

'You can't do this. My father wouldn't believe such a message.'

Pendleton looked at her coldly. 'And why not? He is as anxious as you are that you should become Lady Pendleton. Why shouldn't he believe that you are lunching here with me? He spreads many stories of our association. This one will only be mildly interesting to some I have heard repeated. Besides,' he gave a sneering laugh as he began to close the door after him, 'your father will be too busy preparing to collect his treasure chest to trouble overmuch about his daughter's absence.'

28

Cornelius Tobin cursed the man who handled the boat at the quayside at Liverpool. The night was dark, a fog shrouded the water and land alike, making even a short sea trip a hazardous feat. The boat that he had prepared for the trip swirled and bobbed in the eddying tide.

Tobin was in a black mood. Now that he was crossing to Wallasey to collect the chest from Melany he wondered whether perhaps he was playing into the wreckers' hands. How did he, or Corrina for that matter, know that this girl was not in league with the wreckers. True her tales of what had happened to Jim Grenville since the night the *Golden Lady* had been wrecked seemed convincing enough. If only he or Corrina had actually spoken to Jim Grenville, Tobin felt he would have been easier in his mind.

As he watched the men make final preparations for the trip he wondered again why Corrina had chosen today of all days to take herself off to lunch with Lord Pendleton. Perhaps she thought that by doing so she was helping to keep him out of the way. The thought pleased him and he was still smiling to himself at his daughter's willingness when he felt a sharp tug at his coat sleeve.

'Who is it?' he peered down through the mist and darkness but for the moment he could see no one; then Nabob's voice came to him out of the mist.

'Please, Mister. Missee no can come.'

Irritably Tobin said, 'Come over to the light, Nabob. You're as black as the devil, and on a night like this it is impossible to see you.'

He grasped the black boy's thin arm and half led, half dragged him towards a lantern. He could hear

Nabob's laboured breathing, and he asked sharply, 'Did you run here?'

'Me run all the way, Master. Missee no come. Big Lord not let her.'

In the light of the ship's lantern Tobin looked closer at Nabob. His face was cut and scratched, and his once handsome velvet trousers and silk doublet were dirty and torn.

'What the hell have you been up to, Nabob. You look as if you've been in a fight, or something.'

'Me run all the way, Master. Missee no come. Big Lord not let her.'

'You mean Lord Pendleton?'

'Yes, Master. He not let her come. He shut her in a room.'

'Shut her in a room? What are you talking about.'

'Me don't know. Missie no come. Big Lord won't let her.'

'For God's sake tell me what's wrong.' Angrily Tobin shook the black boy. Nabob's eyes rolled wildly as in terrified tones he began again to gulp out, 'Missie no can come . . . '

'Stop that!' rasped Tobin. 'I understand Miss Corrina can't come. What I want you to tell me is why can't she come here.'

'Big Lord not let her.'

'Lord Pendleton won't let her come.'

'That's right, Master. He shut her in a room.'

'Shut her in a room, what the devil are you on about. Did Miss Corrina send you to tell me all this?'

'No, Master. I slipped through the door, before he locked her and the man in; then I tried to catch up the coach. Big Lord send coach away. I run long way and get lost. When I get home you gone, so I come here and find you.'

Tobin's face was red with anger. Bending down until his face was on a level with the frightened little black boy's he said slowly, 'Nabob good boy. Master pleased with Nabob. Tell Master what else you remember.'

Nabob stood trembling and shaking his black, woolly head.

'Try! Try!' In his desire to make him

speak Tobin clutched his arm tightly. The boy wriggled and whimpered with pain. Releasing him Tobin said, 'Think carefully, Nabob; it is important. This other man who was in the room with Miss Corrina, did they call him Captain Grenville?'

Nabob shook his head slowly. 'No, Master. Missie said 'Jeem'.'

' 'Jeem',' Tobin frowned impatiently. 'You mean Jim?'

'Jeem. Yes, Master, that right, Jeem. Missie said, Jeem, Jeem.'

'So it was Grenville,' muttered Tobin.

'Yes, Master,' agreed Nabob eagerly.

'Can you think of anything else, Nabob.'

The boy shook his dark head. 'No, Master.'

'Try, try, Nabob. What made Lord Pendleton shut Miss Corrina up in a room?'

Nabob's face brightened. 'I tell you that, Master. Missie told big Lord that tonight you go in boat to other side.

Big Lord very cross. Other man tell Missie to be quiet. Big Lord laugh, say he go as well. Say he see you at other side.'

'And then?'

Nabob shrugged expressively. 'Big Lord walk to door, say he shut Missie in room, so I run out. I try to find the carriage but Big Lord talking to coachman and send carriage away. So I run. All through the streets I run; then men chase me . . . '

'Yes, yes, Nabob. You've told me all that before.' He patted the dark woolly head. 'You good boy, Nabob. Come.' He took the boy's hand in his and led him below deck. Here he gave him in charge of one of the men he was taking on the trip.

'Feed the boy,' he instructed. 'And find him something warm to wear.' Then, with a final pat to Nabob's head he returned to the deck.

Standing alone in the darkness he pondered on what action he should take. He paced to and fro debating whether to abandon the scheme and rescue Corrina, or collect the chest first and then storm Pendleton's house. Remembering that Melany would be waiting and if Pendleton turned up she might be led into believing he had been sent to collect the chest, he determined to go ahead with his plans.

As he gave the order to sail Tobin wondered what the outcome of the night's work was to be. He felt the new turn of events boded ill and he wished that he had acquainted the Preventive Officers with the facts as he knew them. With them to back up the twelve men he had recruited success would have been assured. He had held back because of what the chest might contain. He was hoping that the contents would, as Jim Grenville had told Melany, compensate for the loss of the *Golden Lady*.

From the deck he saw the gleam of lights inland getting larger, and brighter, and through the grey swirling mist he could make out the rugged desolate coastline. He hurried to issue last-minute instructions as to where the boat was to be moored.

The seaman listened carefully to the instructions then nodded.

'I know the place you mean, Sir,' he said slowly. ' 'Twill take some manoeuvring to make fast there without beaching the boat.'

'Well beach the boat. There's plenty of you to push her afloat again when we're ready.'

'Might take us a bit longer to get away, that is if we were needing to leave in a hurry.'

Tobin scowled at the man. 'Beach the boat if you must, anchor her if you can, but your instructions are to leave her in the cove.' Without giving the man a chance to answer him he strode away.

Melany was waiting for them wrapped in a dark cloak, the hood of which almost hid her face.

'Bring your men and come quickly,' she told Tobin. 'Tell them not to talk.

There is no knowing who lurks among the sandhills.'

A few yards from the tavern Melany paused and whispered to Tobin, 'Leave a guard here, and post a man at the back of the tavern.' She waited while he briefly instructed two men as to their duties then with her hand on the latch of the nail-studded oak door she again cautioned them.

' 'Twould be better if you came alone to the place where the chest is hidden,' she said to Tobin. 'The sound of many footsteps may easily disturb my aunt.'

Tobin hesitated uneasily. 'One man had better come with me. The chest may be too heavy for me to carry on my own.'

Reluctantly Melany agreed.

Accompanied by one man Tobin followed Melany up the stairs to her room. It was quite dark. Melany, fearful of disturbing her aunt, would not permit so much as a taper or a candle to be used. Tobin had just reached the comparative safety of the landing at the top of the stairs when there was a sudden flare of light. A bedroom door opened and standing there, fully dressed, a lamp in hand, was Mother Redcap.

'It's all right,' Melany told her in a strained voice. 'I can explain everything. This man is . . . '

'We know who he is.' A voice coming from inside the room cut short her explanation. Pushing Mother Redcap aside Matt stood framed in the doorway and behind him, crowding the room, Melany saw seven or eight of his men.

In a flash of fury Tobin rounded on Melany. 'You lying wench,' he cried, 'you are the one in league with the wreckers. I was a fool to listen to your tales. This is a trap you've laid to lure me into their clutches. Much good may it do any of you! By God! If I get out of this lot alive I'll have the Preventive Officers on your tracks and no mistake. As for you, good woman,' he shouted at Mother Redcap, 'I'll see that you are not only put out of business but stoned out of the place into the bargain.'

'Please, please. You must let me speak.' Melany caught at his arm but he pushed her roughly to one side and she would have fallen had not Matt caught her arm and steadied her. Angrily she shook his hand away. 'I will speak,' she insisted. 'I had no idea that Matt had wind of my plans.'

With a twisted smile Matt said, 'What Melany says is quite right, Cornelius Tobin. It was not through Melany, nor Mother Redcap here, that we learnt of your plans for tonight and decided to be here to welcome you.'

'How then did you know of this enterprise,' stormed Tobin. 'God knows we've kept the matter secret enough.'

'Kept it secret!' Matt laughed contemptuously. 'Your daughter in her eagerness to boast to her lover of your achievement, gave us all the information we needed. And very accurate it has proved.'

Tobin smote the clenched fist of one

hand into the palm of the other. 'So that Lily-livered Pendleton is in league with you.'

Matt smiled mockingly. 'Yes, Lord Pendleton and his Reverend Cousin. Now that you are prisoners I feel there is little harm in you knowing this.'

'Your prisoners!'

Matt gave a sneering laugh and indicated the men in the room behind him. 'They are all well armed,' he warned, 'and remember, even if you escaped we still hold Captain Grenville and your daughter. 'Twould be a pity to spoil her pretty looks.'

'You touch, or harm, one hair of my daughter's head . . . '

'And what can you do,' jeered Matt. 'You're a prisoner, our prisoner, just the same as she is. Do what we ask and you will both be set free.'

'And what is it you are hoping I shall do?'

'You'll hand over the chest of treasure that was taken from the *Golden Lady*.'

Tobin sneered contemptuously.

'Do you mean you haven't already taken possession of it?'

Matt shook his head. 'No, we waited for you to lead us to it. Come on. We haven't all night to waste. Hand back the treasure, speak no more about it, and we'll set you and your daughter free.'

'It's not within my power to comply with your instructions. Like you I haven't got the treasure, neither do I know where it is hidden.'

Matt stared at Tobin in silence. Their eyes met and held. Realising that Tobin spoke the truth Matt turned in anger to Melany.

'Well, speak up, where is it hidden?'

'Take your hands off me. I wouldn't give you the treasure if you were to torture me or even kill me.'

'Your talk sounds very brave,' Matt sneered. 'Must be the fine ways you picked up from the Captain when you bedded with him.'

'Keep your evil thoughts to yourself,

Matt. My aunt knows that all I ever did was to nurse Jim Grenville back to health. I'll never betray his secret. Do you hear? Never!'

'The girl speaks the truth, Matt. You've no cause to blacken her name, nor for that matter the name of my tavern. I've always helped anyone in trouble, as you and your men well know, but my tavern has always been held in respect and as long as I am the owner of it, it always shall be.'

'Cut your cackle, woman. If your niece won't give up the treasure, will you?'

Mother Redcap looked round the group of anxious faces slowly. Then she spoke directly to Tobin. 'It seems,' she said at last, 'that unless the treasure is returned to Matt there will be bloodshed here tonight. Shall I hand over the chest to him?'

'But how can you do that, Aunt, you don't know where it is hidden?'

'I know more than you think,' she said quietly. She turned back to Tobin.

'Well, what is your answer?'

For many minutes Tobin stood stroking his chin in anxious thought, then reluctantly, he said, 'Very well. For my daughter's sake, for her safety more than for mine, give it back to these men.'

Matt laughed harshly. 'Very noble sentiments. Lead on, Mother Redcap. Deliver up the treasure and return to your bed.'

'You can't do this!' Horrified Melany tried to stop her aunt.

' 'Tis for the best, child. I know what I'm doing. Stay alongside Mr. Tobin, he will see that no harm befalls you until the deal is completed.'

Tobin placed a hand on Melany's arm. 'You have done your best for Grenville. I will explain all when I see him. These wreckers are wild merciless men, 'tis useless to fight them any more. We will get our revenge someday, never fear. They will not go unpunished.'

Too upset to reply Melany hid her face in his sleeve. Though she made no sound the tears were flowing freely as her aunt took Matt into the bedroom where the chest was hidden.

Tobin's voice was bitter as Matt emerged triumphant. 'Can we go?' Have you finished with us now that you have that.'

'Not so fast. You will come with me and my men. First we will collect the men from your boat, and those you have left guarding this place.'

Surrounded by Matt's men they left the tavern and made for Tobin's boat. Matt detailed four of his men to take charge of it. A sudden cry went up from one of Matt's men and he waved and pointed inland. Some two or three miles away a great beacon had suddenly flared. It filled the night sky as leaping orange tongues of flame danced wildly in the darkness.

With a cry Matt dropped the chest to the ground. 'It's the church,' he yelled. 'It's St. Hilary's church and the vaults are stacked with gunpowder and brandy.'

Even as he spoke there was the dull roar of an explosion that shook the ground beneath their feet. Panic seized the wreckers, they shouted to Matt for instructions, but Matt was looking down at the ground where he had dropped the chest. The others crowded round and for one moment the horror of the fire was wiped from their minds.

In falling the lid of the box had become dislodged. A sprinkling of gold guineas had spewed from the gaping lid. With trembling hands Matt bent to look. Feverishly he tore the lid away, seized the box and tipped its contents onto the sand. In the light of the lanterns held by the men crowding round appeared a pile of pebbles and stones topped by a layer of golden coins.

Hands clenched, Matt viciously kicked at the heap at his feet. The guineas rolled glinting over the sand but the stones remained grey and solid, proof that the wreckers had once again been outwitted.

Trembling, Melany clutched at Tobin's coat and reached out a hand towards her aunt. Mother Redcap appeared outwardly calm but the hand that gripped Melany's was cold and shaking.

'Listen, Melany,' Mother Redcap whispered softly, 'in case we should be parted I want you to know where the treasure is hidden.' Hurriedly she told Melany how she had discovered the treasure after Melany had left the house and gone in search of Tobin. 'I guessed Matt's little game,' she went on. 'The treasure is safe. I've hidden it in an old barrel in a secret passage in the cellar beneath the kitchen floor.'

Conscious that Matt was watching them closely, Melany pressed her aunt's hand to indicate she understood and to silently thank her for her foresight.

29

As the key grated in the lock behind Lord Pendleton, Corrina beat on the door with her fists, imploring him to let her free. She heard his contemptuous laugh and then the dull echo of his footsteps as he walked away from the door. Tears of frustration streamed down her cheeks as she continued to bang on the locked door.

Firmly Grenville took her arm and led her towards a chair. Limply she collapsed into it and gently, as though she was a child, he wiped away her tears.

Now that they were at last alone together he was aghast to find he was completely devoid of emotion or any deep feelings for her.

Throughout his long voyage in the *Golden Lady* and during the time he had spent in hiding over on the

Wallasey side he had ached to be near her. His struggle to outwit the wreckers had been dominated by his desire to right himself in Corrina's eyes. Now, when she was within arms reach, when his blood should have been racing, they were like two strangers.

Instead of being filled with the desire of taking her into his arms he was haunted by the vision of enormous brown eyes set in a solemn oval face.

Even Corrina's tumultuous weeping failed to move him. He stood there beside her, awkwardly patting her golden head.

When she grew calmer he asked what their chances of escape were. Shaking her head dolefully she offered no help so Grenville set about seeking a way out for himself. He examined the windows only to find they were securely barred up. The chimney, though wide, was very dirty and as a fire already burned in the grate it rendered means of escape virtually impossible.

Surely, he reasoned, there must

be some secret means of exit. A man involved in intrigue as Lord Pendleton was would provide himself with some such safeguard. Undaunted, he continued to search. Corrina watched him in bewilderment. He tapped at shelves, took down books and felt along the walls behind them; but no hollow walls responded to his touch. In despair he walked over to the fire-place and moodily leant along the broad mantelpiece. He stood there deep in thought, kicking at a great log that smouldered and crackled in the low hearth. A cry from Corrina made him turn. Her eyes were wide with amazement and he turned to look in the direction she pointed. About three yards from the fireplace, one entire section of the wall, complete with its array of books, was swinging noiselessly inwards. Behind it yawned a dark abyss. Moving towards it Grenville saw a flight of narrow twisting stone steps. He was already down four of them when Corrina protested, 'You can't leave me here, I won't stay. I'm coming with you.'

'It would be better for both of us if you were to stay here,' reasoned Grenville. 'I could travel much faster alone. I might even be in time to warn your father that Pendleton knows of his plans for tonight.'

Stubbornly Corrina stood her ground. 'You can't leave me here on my own,' she protested.

'No harm will come to you,' Grenville told her. 'For one thing Lord Pendleton will be well on his way to Wallasey by now.'

Corrina refused to yield. 'I'm coming with you,' she insisted.

Grenville shrugged. 'Well I warn you the going will be rough, and you're hardly dressed for such a journey.'

Corrida made no answer but clutching her skirts tightly in one hand began to descend the stone stairway.

The steps spiralled downwards ending in a narrow tunnel with uneven floor. Single file they made their way along it, till at last it ended at a door that opened into the stables.

'What are we going to do now?' Corrina asked impatiently.

'See if we can get hold of a horse and ride for the river,' he told her.

'What about warning my father?'

Grenville shook his head. 'It wouldn't be safe. Pendleton may have posted a man to watch the entrance to your home. If we make for the river and manage to get safely across we stand a better chance of helping your father. It is my belief that Pendleton will wait until your father goes to collect the chest before doing anything. It is the treasure Pendleton and the wreckers are so anxious to recover, and they know your father can lead them to it.' Swiftly he harnessed one of the horses and lifted Corrina into the saddle.

'Sit well forward,' he told her. 'I'm coming up behind you. If we take two horses we might easily get parted.'

Swinging into the saddle he touched the horse lightly with his heels; the mare needed no further encouragement, within a matter of minutes they were out onto the open road heading for the river front.

Once safely across the river Corrina, fearing for her father's safety, pleaded that they should go at once to Mother Redcap's and warn Melany that Lord Pendleton knew of their plan. Grenville argued against this.

'Far better that we should go straight to the vicarage.'

'But what good will that do,' asked Corrina tearfully. 'By then the other wreckers, led by Matt, may have already killed my father.'

Grenville shook his head. 'I think not,' he said. 'Matt would not have the authority to do that. I think it is more likely that Matt and his men will wait until Melany has handed over the treasure then round up your father and his men and bring them to Lord Pendleton and the vicar. Matt is just a ruffian and even if he did manage to get the treasure from your father it would be of no use to him. It will take some very clever negotiating to dispose of the contents of that chest without arousing suspicion. Since they have waited so long to move the chest, we may even be lucky enough to intercept the men who were to take the contents from Lord Pendleton.'

'But what good will all that do us,' wailed Corrina. 'All I want to do is to see my father safe. I care nothing for the treasure. I wish I had never heard of it.'

Grenville patted her arm consolingly. 'Tonight will see the end of the matter. One way, or the other, we shall know our fate within the next few hours. If you wish you may still return home to Liverpool.

Corrina shook her head and clutched at his arm. 'No!' she protested, 'you can't send me back.'

Grenville said no more but taking her hand set off at a steady pace towards St. Hilary's church.

30

Herded like cattle, Melany, Mother Redcap and Tobin were taken by Matt and his men through the Red Nose Caves.

It was a wearying journey. Matt was surly and impatient. His men, reflecting his humour, pushed and prodded their prisoners, in an effort to make them walk more quickly over the narrow uneven path. Unused to the caves Tobin and his party constantly tore their clothes, and bruised themselves against the rugged sides.

Mile after endless mile they trudged, footsore and fearful of what lay in store for them at the end of the journey.

Gradually the air inside the cave became acrid with smoke fumes. In a flash it came to Tobin's mind that they were heading for the vaults of the church, walking straight into their own funeral pyre. Alarmed, he called to Matt, 'Have you forgotten the church is on fire.'

Matt flashed him a contemptuous look. 'Do you think you are the only man alive who can think,' he taunted. 'Is it likely that I would march you all to certain death? Little as I value your life, and that of your accomplices, I have some care for my own and that of my men.'

Even as he spoke they reached a point where the cave divided. Matt led his men and prisoners along a fork to the left. Within a few hundred yards the air became cleaner.

They stopped at a door which Matt opened with a key taken from his pocket. As they filed through they found themselves in a large empty cellar.

Locking the door behind them Matt led them up a flight of stone steps which led into the vicarage. Here, he knocked loudly on a heavy oak door to the right of the hall and a woman answered immediately.

'Vicar set off for the church two hours ago. He said to tell you to follow him.' She regarded him anxiously, 'I've been at my wits end to know what to do. The church is on fire and I fear lest some harm has come to him.'

'Was he alone when he left the house?' Matt asked sharply.

'Alone, no! Lord Pendleton was with him. Both of them seemed in a mighty stir about something.'

Once more Matt's men poked and prodded their prisoners into action.

As they emerged from the vicarage an appalling sight met their eyes. Five hundred yards to their right lay the church, a gigantic furnace outlined by leaping flames. A crowd of villagers were as close to the red, roaring inferno as they dared go. No one attempted to appease the burning.

The housekeeper, who had followed them to the door, gasped out, ' 'Tis the will God! 'Tis his revenge for the terrible things that goes on hereabouts.

'Tis God's warning I tell you!'

Roughly Matt pushed the woman to one side and strode towards the church. In the graveyard he jostled with the villagers, pushing them roughly aside with his elbows.

'No good trying to get in,' warned a man. 'There's folks trapped inside as it is.'

'Who is trapped inside?' Matt seized the man's arm in a powerful twist. 'Who is in there?' he hissed.

The man rubbed at his bruised arm. 'Vicar's in there, and some others.'

'But who are the others,' persisted Matt, impatiently.

'Lord Pendleton is probably in there with him,' interrupted Tobin.

Matt turned on him in rage. 'Be quiet!' he snarled.

He turned back to the man he had been questioning. 'Well?'

'Vicar's in there and two other men and a woman; we heard her screaming.'

In a flash Tobin was at the man's side. Delving into his pockets he brought out a handful of money — crowns, half sovereigns and gold guinea pieces — cramming them into the man's hands he pleaded, 'Think carefully, what else can you tell us.'

The man looked at the fistful of money in awe. Then struggling to remember he said slowly, 'The woman was young and had yellow hair. When I first got here the fire was raging along the nave of the church. She rushed to the north door, there was a man by her side, a tall red-headed man. They made as if to run from the church but the vicar and the man with him pulled them back. 'Twas then that the girl screamed.'

Heedless of the cries of the crowd, Melany ran towards the blazing inferno.

'Stop her!' bellowed Tobin, then as she battled on, through the smoke and heat, made after her.

The man to whom Tobin had given the money tried to stop him but Matt pushed the man aside.

'Let him go, if he has a mind to,' he

said. 'He may as well die that way as any other. The girl you spoke of was his daughter.'

The man stared at Matt in horror. 'And that young dark girl . . . '

Matt shrugged. 'The redheaded man inside the church is her lover.'

31

The wind carried the flames towards the sea and although the nave burnt like a November bonfire the church tower, the north door and porch remained unscarred. The air there, although acrid with smoke, and scorching from the heat of the fire, was still bearable.

Crouched inside the porch Tobin and Melany found the vicar, Lord Pendleton, Grenville and Corrina.

'For God's sake leave this place. Any minute now and the main part of the building will collapse,' warned Tobin.

The vicar laughed, shrilly.

'We knew Matt was bringing you,' Pendleton said, 'that's why we waited. Where is he now?'

'Standing just outside.'

Pendleton sneered. 'Matt always was just a little cautious to my way of thinking. He should have delivered you into our hands personally.'

'Matt doesn't even know you are still alive.' Tobin made as if to take Corrina's arm but the vicar pushed him to one side.

'You must excuse your daughter's lack of greeting,' he sneered, 'but if you look closer you will see we have taken the precaution of gagging her. Like most women she screams when she is frightened, and she frightens easily.'

'You swine!' breathed Tobin.

Turning to the vicar Pendleton said, 'Shouldn't you explain that both Miss Tobin and the Captain are trussed up ready to go on the bonfire before you and I leave.'

'My God! You'll pay for this.' A vein pulsed angrily in Tobin's florid brow. 'If I leave this place alive I'll see you're both punished for your part in this affair.'

'If any of us leave this place alive,' mocked the vicar.

'If any of us do I rather think it will

be the vicar and I, so who will there be to punish us?'

Pendleton's question hung unanswered on the smoke-laden air. He shrugged and went on, 'As far as the treasure is concerned, has it been returned to us?'

'Oh, no!' Tobin spoke triumphantly. 'Matt found the chest but the treasure in it had been replaced by pebbles and stones.'

Anger contorting his face, Pendleton moved towards Melany.

Tobin stood between them. 'You'll not touch the girl,' he said.

Pendleton's eyes narrowed as he stepped back. 'Perhaps when she feels it growing a little warmer she will be more prepared to help us. Make no mistake, no one leaves here until we know where the treasure is hidden.'

'Well?' Pendleton turned threateningly to Melany. 'Are you going to tell us where the contents of the chest have gone?'

Over Pendleton's shoulder Melany saw

Grenville shake his head emphatically.

Tobin looked from one face to the other in blank dismay. The air around them was growing hotter and the acrid smoke parched his throat and tongue.

While indecision hung in the air as thick and heavy as the smoke, there was a sudden scuffle, then a thud, and in a moment a general melee followed.

Corrina had managed to wriggle free from the bonds that secured her hands and ankles and had thrown herself at the vicar; grasping him around the throat from behind. Overpowered by the sudden attack he fell to the ground, his head hitting the stone floor with such force that he was stunned.

Without a moment's hesitation Tobin flung himself upon Pendleton, wrestling with the younger man as though possessed, until Pendleton, too, lay inert on the ground.

Melany seized the opportunity to free Grenville from the cords binding his hands and ankles.

Seeing that there was no need to help

Tobin, Grenville pulled Melany into his arms. They clung together oblivious of what was happening around them until a scream from Corrina startled them all. The vicar no longer lay senseless on the ground. Supporting himself with a chair he stood knife in hand, his arm upraised and poised for a deadly thrust into Grenville's back. Surprised by Corrina's scream he turned, then in a frenzied fury he lunged at her and the knife sank to the hilt between her ribs.

Grenville was at Corrina's side instantly. Tears filled Melany's eyes as she saw him drop to his knees beside the lifeless body and gently kiss Corrina's brow. It was a kiss filled with finality, a kiss of farewell to one he had once known and loved dearly. Her heart ached for him. The jealousy she had once felt withered within her.

Melany turned away and watched as the flames licked hungrily over the dry stonework. She watched in awe as a smouldering mass of masonry sent sparks soaring into the night sky. She looked back to where Jim was rising from Corrina's side to make way for Cornelius Tobin. Gently Tobin lifted the limp body and began to walk towards the door. As he did so a shower of red hot sparks came from the roof as the fire grew more intense.

'Run for it, Grenville,' Tobin ordered. 'Get Melany out before the roof collapses.

She made no move until she felt Grenville's arm around her shoulders. As she turned to face him he pulled her towards him, crushing her against his chest. 'It's all over now,' he murmured, burying his face in her hair. 'It's like wakening from a harrowing dream. The fire has cleansed all the evil away.'

Gently he raised her face, his grey eyes were warm and tender, yet at the same time questioning. 'Can we forget the past?' he asked. 'Can we build a new future together?'

In the red glow that suffused the building he read the answer in her eyes.

His arm still holding her protectively he led her to safety. Eager hands reached out to them as they emerged from the church. Behind them they heard the ominous rumblings as the porch crumbled beneath the fire's intense heat.

'I love you, Melany,' he whispered. 'I'll even give up the sea if you'll marry me.'

Melany's eyes misted as she shook her head. 'The sea is your life,' she told him.

'You're my life,' he insisted. 'Will you marry me, whatever my future may be?'

'Yes!' she told him without hesitation. 'Without you I'd have no future.'

Their lips met in a long, tender kiss, sealing their vows to each other. For a brief moment they were oblivious to everything except their overwhelming love for each other. Their joy in being together and their hopeful anticipation for the future, enveloped them like a protective cloak. Their absorption in each other was suddenly shattered, however, as a wild unearthly scream rent the air. A figure appeared surrounded by a halo of flames, a human torch screaming with pain and terror, before falling in a smouldering heap to the ground.

In the awful silence that followed a man's voice spoke from the crowd.

' 'Tis the vicar himself. 'Tis God's judgement on his unholy ways.'

Of the church, only a burning shell remained. The Tower was still erect, pointing menacingly upwards into the night sky, a warning finger.

THE END

We do hope that you have enjoyed reading this large print book.

Did you know that all of our titles are available for purchase?

We publish a wide range of high quality large print books including:

Romances, Mysteries, Classics
General Fiction
Non Fiction and Westerns

Special interest titles available in large print are:

The Little Oxford Dictionary
Music Book, Song Book
Hymn Book, Service Book

Also available from us courtesy of Oxford University Press:

Young Readers' Dictionary
(large print edition)
Young Readers' Thesaurus
(large print edition)

For further information or a free brochure, please contact us at:

Other titles in the Linford Romance Library:

DREAM OF A DOCTOR

Lynne Collins

Melissa had discarded a sentimental dream of the attractive doctor who had inspired her to train as a nurse. However, his unexpected return to the hospital meant that she was constantly reminded of a fateful weekend. And so was Luke, for very different reasons. Time hadn't healed the damage done to his heart by her beautiful cousin, Julie, who Melissa knew he still loved. So it would be foolish to allow a dream to be revived when it could never come true.

A SUMMER FOLLY

Peggy Loosemore Jones

Philippa Southcott was a very ambitious musician. When she gave a recital on her harp in the village church she met tall, dark-haired Alex Penfold, who had recently inherited the local Manor House, and couldn't get him out of her mind. Philippa didn't want anything or anyone to interfere with her career, least of all a man as disturbing as Alex, but keeping him at a distance turned out to be no easy matter!

THE DARK DRUMS

Anna Martham

Anona Trent is engaged by Jermyn St Croix as governess to his daughter at his plantation home on the island of Saint-Domingue in the Caribbean. At Casabella, Anona discovers there is a secret connected with the death of Jermyn's wife, Melanie, and that Jermyn himself is cold and forbidding. Before long, Anona finds herself falling in love with a man who tells her he can never return her love, and on the exotic island she finds both mystery and despair.